# Steampunk Holmes: Legacy of the Nautilus

D1091299

**Written By P. C. Martin**

Concept, Richard Monson-Haefel
Illustrations, Daniel Cortes
Cover, John Coulthart

Published by Noble Beast, LLC
And MX Publishing

Paperback ISBN  9781780922461

Published in the UK by MX Publishing
335 Princess Park Manor, Royal Drive,
London, N11 3GX
www.mxpublishing.com

Grateful acknowledgment to Conan Doyle Estate Ltd. for
permission to use the Sherlock Holmes characters created by the
late Sir Arthur Conan Doyle.

# Acknowledgements

P.C. Martin, Daniel Cortes, and Richard Monson-Haefel of Noble Beast, LLC. would like to thank our 1,290 Kickstarter Backers who helped to make this project successful. Among those sponsors are the Diamond and Gold Level Sponsors who contributed the most to our campaign.

| Diamond Level Backers | Gold Level Backers |
| --- | --- |
| David W. Kaufman II | Robert Gould |
| Michael Hunger | Phelan Trautmann |
| Amy Evans | Andrew Lechner |
| Chris Nichols | Mary Lou Haefel |
| John Idlor | Faye Donaya Haymond |
| David Swallow | Peter Spicer |
| Don Meares | Brett Wilson |
| Ryan James | Marlo Botman |
| Ann O'Nimity | Scott Wakefield |
| | Tim Reich |
| | Kay-Lynn Cavanagh |
| | Andy Bates |
| | Paul Selby |
| | Christopher Lau |
| | David Kickbusch |
| | Dustin Ambler |
| | James R. Hall |
| | James Fryer |
| | Owen Spendlove |
| | Derik Porvaznik |
| | David Lamme |

# Table of Contents

# Sherlock Holmes

# Chapter One

When I look over my case notes, I find that the early weeks of the year 1885 are prominently recorded as having been nearly devoid of those little problems which so fascinated my friend Sherlock Holmes. However, there began in that year a series of cases which quickly proved to be of the most fantastic and unbelievable nature, to the extent that I hesitate to write them down for fear that my sanity will be put in question. To my friend Sherlock Holmes and myself, these all began with the tragedy surrounding the case of the disappearance of the Nautilus submarine plans—though this proved to be merely a prelude, and that comparatively humble, to a sea of bizarre happenings which fully occupied our time and energies for many months to follow, and which taxed even my friend's singular powers to their very limits.

I have been constrained not to publish any account of this case and its strange sequels, for deep political intrigues were involved, and woven through the seams, lengthwise and cross, were state secrets of most sensitive importance. Indeed, though I cannot ever hope to thrill a long-suffering public with even a modest disclosure of that strange series of events, I feel compelled, nevertheless, to write a factual account of these cases, in which my friend Holmes and I took part, and although these documents must afterwards be padlocked and sealed in my private journal, I pray that some day, the knowledge I am about to disclose may be of beneficial service to some worthy soul.

I awoke one dank February morning to find Sherlock Holmes standing fully dressed, by the side of my bed. He was a late riser, as a rule, and as the clock on the mantelpiece showed me that it was only a quarter-past seven, I blinked up at him in some surprise, and perhaps just a little resentment, for I was myself regular in my habits.

"Very sorry to wake you up, Watson," said he, "but it's the common lot this morning. Mrs. Hudson has been woken up, she retorted upon me, and I on you."

"What is it, then—a fire?"

"No; a telegram from my sister Mycroft," replied Holmes, "which promises to be of exceptional interest. Mycroft never sends for me except in cases of the most baffling nature, and I thought you might rather accompany me."

"Certainly I would," cried I, leaping from my pillow and splashing my face from the basin in the corner.

"Excellent, then; have some coffee before we go. I'll get my coat and start up the Widow."

I winced at the prospect. Holmes' enormous motorized bicycle, the Widowmak'r, was his pet hobby, and so enamored was he with its power and terrific capability for speed, he could not keep his enjoyment of the vehicle to himself. The Widowmak'r got its name from the engineer Holmes employed to help him build it. The engineer, a cankerous old man but a genius with $H_2O_2$ steam engines, told Holmes that no good could come of such a machine. He called it a "Widowmak'r" because it would surely kill Holmes and leave his wife a widow. Holmes had laughed at that, and said he had no intention of ever marrying, but he immediately fancied the name Widowmak'r – or Widow for short – and has used it ever since.

As I had shown great unwillingness to ride pillion on the monstrous machine, Holmes had contrived a marvelous side-car in order that I might share in the excitement of the Widow's adventurous sallies in what he called perfect safety. I had been flattered by this excessive kindness on my friend's part, until about ten seconds had elapsed on my first ride in the Widow's side-car.

In defense of my own courage, I have been shot at, stabbed, and seen my own arm torn from my body upon the hostile battlefields of India and Afghanistan, and yet none of those terrors compare in my estimation with that of driving through London with Holmes at the helm. After that momentous and traumatizing inaugural ride, my mistrust of the vehicle had grown to a positive terror—less for the vehicle's sake than for my friend's tempestuous and unbelievably reckless driving skills.

This morning my mechanical arm felt clumsier than usual as I shaved and dressed, and gulped down my coffee and a scone. I scraped my brains for an argument which might dissuade Holmes from driving the Widow to the appointment with his sister.

Holmes was already seated expectantly upon the machine, wearing driving gloves and goggles, when I descended into the basement garage. Resolutely, I shouted over the rumbling din of the Widow's powerful motor.

"Couldn't we take a cab, Holmes?"

Holmes shook his head. "Too slow," he said, handing me my helmet. I sighed and tried again.

"The train, then? I really must confess, Holmes, I'm feeling a trifle under the weather today..."

"Capital!" shouted Holmes, before I had quite finished. "A leisurely drive through London to the Ministry will do for you beautifully. Hop in, Watson, and strap up well!"

I shook my head and climbed, with the greatest of reluctance, into my appointed space, and found that the compartment had shrunk considerably since my last ride in the side-car.

"Holmes? What have you got in here? My legs hardly fit."

"Oh, just a minor feature or two I've added recently. Pay no mind to it."

I had scarce settled myself when the garage door slid open with a clang and we shot out into the foggy London air.

Twenty minutes later found us in the environs of the Ministry where Mycroft Holmes had her office. Holmes parked the Widow some several hundred yards away in a sheltered and well-policed lane, and I clambered out of my confines with unsteady legs and trembling hands, immeasurably grateful that we had reached the end of the journey unharmed.

As we walked through muddy slush towards the Ministry building, I remarked bitterly on the dreary weather, and Holmes, correctly interpreting my thoughts, smiled.

"I assure you, Watson, knowing Mycroft as I do, that our small sacrifices this morning will be amply rewarded by the divine complexity of the puzzle she will lay before us. "

"By the way, Watson," said Holmes abruptly, "have you any idea what Mycroft is?"

"You once told me that she holds some small office under the British government."

"Bless you, Watson," Holmes laughed, "I suppose I did not know you well then. One must always be cautious when speaking about state affairs. But I believe it is fair to say that Mycroft occasionally *is* the British government."

"My dear Holmes!"

"I thought that might surprise you. My sister Mycroft is the most unambitious person in all of England. She has extensive authority and draws a small fortune annually; yet she will never receive honor nor title if she can possibly avoid it, for she abhors publicity of any kind. That said, Mycroft is by far the most indispensable person in the Empire."

"But how?"

"Sister Mycroft has the greatest brain of our time, Watson, with a limitless capacity for storing facts. Those same powers that I have employed in the detection of crime, she has put to use for the government, and has created for herself a unique position in which to employ her peculiar and marvelous talents. She receives the conclusions of each department, and acts as a central exchange or clearing-house, balancing all factors and decisions made between one and another. All men are specialists; her specialism is omniscience. Supposing a Minister requires information involving the Navy, China, the West trade, and the bimetallic engineering question; he would get his separate advices from the various departments, but only Mycroft could say how each factor would affect the other. Again and again her word has decided the national policy. She has on numerous occasions, to my certain knowledge, been highly commended by her Majesty the Queen herself."

I was suitably impressed by my friend's description of his illustrious sister, of whom I had only heard Holmes speak once some years before.

"Here," continued Holmes, "why don't you read her wire aloud and see what you make of it; the name she refers to recalls nothing to my mind." He handed me the telegram, and I read,

'Must see you over Cadbury. Come at once.'

I shook my head doubtfully. "Well, it couldn't possibly be the chocolate confectioners, could it?" said I.

"I hardly think so," Holmes chuckled. "Sister Mycroft's influence is most unlikely to extend into the realm of sweets. Anyway, it is evident that this Cadbury must be a person of supreme importance, since Mycroft is concerned."

He took up the note and scrutinized it intently, as though searching for missing clues within its lines, as we approached the massive Ministry, and walked up the steps to the entrance hall.

At the door Holmes exhibited Mycroft's telegram to the guard at the latter's request, and then we proceeded to the lift, ascended to the third floor, and were ushered into an imposing office.

Mycroft Holmes rose with alacrity from behind an enormous rosewood desk, and came forward to greet us as Holmes introduced me. As all mention of Mycroft's appearance had entirely escaped Holmes' description of her, I had vaguely formed a mental picture of a stern, imperious feminine replica of my friend.

In fact, at first sight Mycroft Holmes was almost disturbingly beautiful; tall, statuesque in figure, graceful in motion, and possessed of a subtle element of quiet charm. But in her attractive face I recognized the alert steel-gray eyes and the keenness of expression that I knew so well in my friend Holmes, and vividly called to my attention the dominant mind that commanded such influence over the affairs of the Empire.

Near the window stood our old friend Inspector Lestrade of Scotland Yard. His grave, austere face was more solemn than usual as he shook hands with Holmes and me in turn.

"I see that it is not necessary to introduce the Inspector," said Mycroft Holmes, settling herself in a huge leather chair. "This business is dreadfully annoying, Sherlock, and such bad timing, in the present condition of Siam. The Admiralty is in such a state, and good heavens, the Prime Minister! I have never seen him so upset."

"Ghastly," agreed Holmes. "Perhaps you will give us the facts, dear sister Mycroft?"

"The facts, yes. Have you ever heard of the Nautilus submarine?"

Holmes shook his head. I started, surprised, for the name was somehow familiar to me. Miss Holmes' eyes narrowed. "You know of it, Doctor Watson?"

"I think I have heard the name," replied I. "It is vaguely connected in my memory with my campaign in India, though I cannot place it exactly."

Mycroft Holmes breathed as though with relief. "Excellent. This submarine—or rather the plans for its construction—has been the most jealously guarded of all government secrets. Perhaps I had better give you a brief sketch of its history. The submarine was developed some twenty years ago by a renegade Northern Indian prince calling himself Captain Nemo, who used the vessel to cause considerable headaches among the international shipping routes. By providence the Captain and his ship were reported as lost several years ago. Two years ago, to be exact, we learned of its location under the seas, and a top-secret expedition was dispatched to seek out and recover the ship, and learn its secrets. According to the reports submitted to me at the time, the vessel, when discovered , was too damaged to be moved, so the party was obliged to study and document its every detail sub undis. When the observations were completed, the ship was blasted to oblivion. Meticulous plans were drawn for its reconstruction, and special Engine cards were created for the purpose of storing the vital information. These were kept in an elaborate strongroom in a confidential office adjoining the Woolwich Arsenal, and never removed from the premises. If the chief Navy constructor desired to consult them, even he was constrained to go personally to the office in Woolwich."

Mycroft paused in her narrative, and Holmes half-opened his eyes. "The plans have been stolen, I see," he mumbled. "Who is Cadbury, and what has he to do with the matter?"

I looked, astonished, towards my friend, who was leaning placidly with his elbows on the arms of his chair and his fingertips joined together. Inspector Lestrade appeared to share my astonishment; Mycroft Holmes did not seem disturbed.

"Cadbury was the junior clerk employed in the Woolwich Arsenal office. Early this morning, he was found dead beside a London railway line, with seven of the ten Engine cards in his pockets. The three most essential cards are vanished, and we have not the slightest clue where they are. It is wretched, absolutely wretched, from an official standpoint! You must drop everything, Sherlock; never mind all your petty puzzles and intrigues for the moment. This is a vital international problem, and I can hardly exaggerate its importance."

"What are the risks?" queried Holmes.

"The technology of the submarine's weaponry and power generator is far advanced for its time. The missing cards show detailed schematics of the power generator – a technology so sophisticated and mysterious that our best engineers have not been able to completely discern its workings. The weaponry itself is so powerful that Naval warfare becomes impossible within the radius of a Nautilus operation. If the plans were to fall into the wrong hands ..." Mycroft Holmes left off speaking and shook her head with utmost solemnity.

Holmes' eyes opened slightly again. "You begin to interest me," said he. "Who is officially responsible for the plans?"

"Sir James Valentine, the son of a distinguished officer in the Afghanistan War. I see that Dr. Watson knows of him."

"Indeed I do," I replied, nodding heartily. "I had the honor of briefly serving with Colonel Hugh Valentine's regiment in '78, just before his death."

"Sir James was instrumental in locating the lost submarine and drafting its plans," continued Mycroft. "He oversaw the financing of the expedition, and managed the research of the Nautilus for the Navy."

"Pray, go on," said Holmes. "Who had access to the strongroom?"

"Sir James himself kept a set of keys," said Mycroft, "and Sidney Johnson, the senior clerk and draftsman, kept the only other set. I may add that the plans were undoubtedly in the office during working hours on Monday, and Sir James left the office during the early afternoon, taking his keys with him. By the by, he was summoned to meet us here. How deuced odd that he has not yet arrived."

"Indeed," said Holmes. "Perhaps he did not have the good sense to take the train. These new-fangled gurneys crowding the streets these days are enough to prevent anyone from arriving at one's destination at all. But do continue. Who was the last to see the cards?"

"Mr. Johnson locked up the cards for the night while the office staff prepared to depart, and was the last to leave the office, according to all accounts. He claims to have been at home with his family during the whole of the evening, and Lestrade's men are even now verifying his statements. He has a wife and five children, to whom he is apparently devoted, and is known to be a man of retiring disposition when not in the office. A dour-faced man, not very popular among his colleagues, yet hitherto steady and trustworthy. For my part, I would be intensely surprised to learn that Sidney Johnson had anything to do with the events of last night."

"I presume the office is well guarded?" queried Holmes.

"The office is equipped with burglar-proof windows and doors; the grounds are well lit, and patrolled by trained guards, mainly old soldiers, all of whom have proven their loyalty time and again. Mr. Johnson had not yet discovered the loss of the cards when Lestrade approached him this morning about the death of his junior clerk, and the presence of the cards on his person. They verified that the strong-room had indeed been bereft of its most valuable contents, and Lestrade notified me at once."

"The guards had neither seen nor heard anything during the night?"

"Not a soul of them. There was, however, a dense fog, which would have effectively prevented them from seeing their fingertips at arm's-length, much less a thief slipping silently through the door."

"I see. Tell me more about Cadbury."

"He was one of the finest Engine programmers in the service, and had done excellent work at the office for over ten years; he had the reputation of being a sound, honest man, though perhaps a trifle hot-headed. His duties brought him into daily contact with the cards."

"He did not possess a key to the strongroom?"

"No; though the possibility that he had a duplicate must be considered."

"Was such a key found on his person?"

Lestrade found his voice for the first time. "No, the only key we found was the key to his rooms. There were no signs of robbery about his person; all his possessions were intact, except for the missing cards."

Holmes smiled kindly at the inspector, and resumed questioning his sister.

"What would the value of the cards be, assuming that he intended to sell them?"

"He could have gotten several thousands for them very easily."

"That is settled, then. How did he meet his death?"

Again, Lestrade answered at Mycroft's silent prompting. "He was found early this morning by a railway plate-layer named Mason, just outside Aldgate Station on the Underground system in

London. His head was badly crushed—an injury we suspect was caused by a fall from the train."

"What else was on his person, besides the key to his rooms?" inquired Holmes.

"Well, he had about two pounds fifteen, in loose change; a Monetary card issued by the Woolwich branch of the Capital and Counties Bank, through which his identity was established. There were also two dress-circle tickets for the Woolwich Theater, dated for that very evening."

"Only two pounds—I see. Not the spectacular sum one might expect for the sale of the three missing cards. Interesting. Did he have a train ticket?"

"No sir, none that we could find."

Holmes sat upright. "No train ticket! That is really singular. If I am not mistaken, the lines near the station at Aldgate run mostly Metropolitan trains, and it is my experience that it is not possible to reach the platform on a Metropolitan line without necessarily exhibiting one's ticket. It is indeed remarkable. I presume all trains and carriages were searched?"

"Yes, Mr. Holmes; first thing this morning. My lads are still at work, but so far, we haven't found a thing to help us discover where the young man came from, where he was headed, or how he met his death."

"I see," said Holmes again, leaning back into his chair. "Well, sister Mycroft, there are points of interest in this case, but I do not see how I can be of much use to you. If the plans were stolen last night, as seems to be the case, then regardless of how it was accomplished and for what reason, the obvious result would appear to be that the cards are even now in the hands of whoever sought to acquire them. Perhaps they are already on the continent. What is there for us to do?"

"To act, Sherlock—to act!" cried Miss Holmes, pounding on the desk with both fists. "All my instincts are against this explanation. Use your powers! Go to the scene of the crime! See the people concerned! Leave no stone unturned! In your entire career you have never had so great a chance of serving your country. If you ever had any fancy to find your name on the next honors list--"

"Not I," Holmes smiled and shook his head. "I play the game for the game's sake. But Mycroft, surely your own powers are at least equal, if not superior, to mine. Why not solve the case yourself?"

"It's a question of details, Sherlock. Give me all the details, and I will solve the matter right here in my office. But running here and there, cross-questioning railway guards, and lying on my face with a lens to my eye—these are not my métier. No, you are the one who can clear the matter up, brother Sherlock. I know that once you are put onto a scent, you will follow it till its end. May we count on you to help us?"

Holmes shrugged. "I shall look into the matter. Come along, Watson. Lestrade, if you will favor us with your company for an hour or two, perhaps you can enlighten us in all the minor details of the case. Good-bye, Mycroft; you'll receive my report before evening, though I warn you that you may expect little."

We had hardly left the Ministry building when a frantic page shouted Holmes' name, and rushed out after us in a flurry of askew collars and flushed cheeks. Holmes, frowning at the disheveled youth, took up the note and tore it open as the messenger turned and fled back up the steps into the building.

"What is it, Holmes?" I asked anxiously, for the color deepened in Holmes' face, and his eyes held the telling glint of the hound upon a scent.

"The matter grows graver," replied he with a grim smile, handing the note to Lestrade. "Kindly read it aloud, Lestrade?"

The inspector's eyebrows rose, and a low whistle escaped his lips. "It's from Miss Holmes," said he. "'Have just received notice of Sir James Valentine's death by suicide this morning.' But this is awful, Mr. Holmes! What can it possibly mean?"

"I'm afraid it can only mean one of a few things," replied my friend. "But we mustn't lose time in idle speculations, Lestrade; our work is cut out for us. Let us first repair to the station where young Cadbury's body was found, and from there we can proceed to investigate the matter of his employer's death. Come Watson; we shall take the train with Lestrade, and return for the Widow later."

Despite the dim, foggy weather and the somber task before us, my heart gave a silent leap for joy at the prospect of leaving the Widowmak'r behind.

# Doctor Watson

# Chapter Two

On our way to the station, the inspector, at Holmes' prompting, provided further details regarding the deceased Cadbury.

"Well, now, let me see," Lestrade scrutinized the pages of his pocket notebook. "He was an only son, living with his widowed mother, Madame Cadbury, in a small house near Woolwich."

"Soon to be married, I understand?"

"He was engaged to a Miss Victoria Valentine; the sister, in fact, of Sir James Valentine."

Holmes took in this information with a severe frown. "How informative, Lestrade. Can the young lady account at all for her fiancé's actions of the evening?"

"She was officially informed this morning of her fiancé's death, but no statement was taken at the time. We are, of course, seeing directly to the interrogation of the young man's immediate family and associates." Lestrade puffed out his breath in characteristic pompous fashion.

"Well, I shall direct my attention thither immediately after we finish our examination of the place where the body was found," said Holmes. "Perhaps Miss Valentine or Madame Cadbury can shed some light on our little problem. Ah, here we are at Aldgate, if I am not much mistaken."

Two men met us on the platform; one red-faced elderly representative of the railway company, and a man whom I judged to be a plain-clothed policeman. The old gentleman courteously led the way to the spot where the body had lain. Holmes' quick eye swept over every detail of the scene before us. A chalked body mark lay about nine feet to the left of an outward curve in the rails, not a hundred yards from the station. Holmes examined the mark and rails with great care, his powerful lens close to the ground.

"Barely a trace or two of clotted blood where the body landed, still less where he rolled to a halt," he remarked. "Not much bleeding, I see."

"No," replied the plain-clothes, with something of a shudder, "there was a terrific wound to the head, but the doctor supposed that the hemorrhage must have been mainly internal. It was a most ghastly sight."

"Certainly there was some blood on his person, though?" I asked, with some surprise, recalling the many head wounds I had treated on the battlefields of Afghanistan.

"Well yes, there was, His head and jacket collar were drenched in blood."

"Odd," said I, "that there is so little blood on the ground, in such a case."

"Did the trains reveal no sign of violence?" asked Holmes, peering up at us from his crouched position.

"None whatever that we could find," replied Lestrade. "We searched every carriage that went through this station last night."

Holmes' eyes narrowed to a slit, and I saw on his keen, alert face that tightening of the lips, that quiver of the nostrils which I knew so well, the signals that he was intent on a chase. He drew himself up and gazed about us.

High blank walls flanked the tracks on either side of the area where we stood; wires crossed high overhead; a junction of switches a few yards from the chalked area suddenly caught Holmes' attention, and upon these he fixed himself with eagerness.

"I suppose there are no great number of switches such as these on this particular system of lines?"

"No, sir," replied the elderly gentleman. Holmes' eyes glinted, and his voice betrayed suppressed excitement.

"And an outbound curve, too. By Jove! If it were only so! And yet, why not?"

"Have you a clue, Mr Holmes?" queried Lestrade with some surprise.

"An idea—nothing more. It may lead to nothing. But the case grows every moment in interest. Come Watson, let us be gone; I have seen all I wanted to see here. Good-bye, Lestrade; we need not trouble you further for the present, I believe. Our investigations must now carry us to Woolwich."

Holmes sent a telegram to Mycroft Holmes from the station before boarding the train to Woolwich. It ran,

"See possible light in darkness. Please immediately send by messenger to Baker Street complete list of all known foreign spies and international agents residing in London, with full address."

Holmes and I took our seats opposite one other in the Woolwich train. His manner betrayed the fact that the wheels of his brain were spinning furiously, tracing a complex chain from some elusive clue that had entirely escaped me, and most likely Lestrade as well. He lounged, apathetic and contemplative, in his seat; the next moment he started violently, just as we emerged from a tunnel, and craning his head, gazed earnestly out the window at the sky; a few moments later he resigned himself to his seat with restless fingers and tapping feet, until at last he sank back into a meditative reverie with half-closed lids.

I knew him too well to expect an answer to any direct question when he was in such a mood, but at last my curiosity overcame me.

"What is it, Holmes?" I asked. My friend started.

"It is only an idea, Watson. The more I reflect upon it, the stranger it seems even to me, and yet it would fit the facts so beautifully if it were true. Why was the body found near a junction of switches, just as the line curves towards Aldgate? It must have been thrown from a train, and yet why was his ticket not found?"

"Why not indeed?" I asked, puzzled. "Has that so great a bearing upon the case?"

"Certainly it does, my dear Watson. I do not have all the facts yet to solve the greater mystery of the theft, but before we investigate the question of how the cards were taken and why they were found on Cadbury's person—if indeed he did not take them himself—we must ascertain how his body came to land in such a strange location. When we have discovered that, the rest of the pieces must fall into place."

"Perhaps," I conjectured, "he stole the cards, and brought them to whomever he intended to sell them to. The cards were sold, and as Cadbury returned to the station with his loot, he was followed by that same agent, who boarded his carriage, killed him, took back the money he had paid for the cards, removed the ticket to conceal the station from which they came, and replaced the seven cards that he judged least crucial to his purpose in the dead man's pocket. He then threw the body out of the train just as the train curved toward Aldgate station, making it appear as an accident, or suicide."

"Excellent, Watson! It is a fine theory you put forth, and I must congratulate you. It is true that you omitted most of the noteworthy details of the crime, but it was a splendid attempt at reconstruction, nevertheless."

I frowned, a trifle offended at his withering criticism. "What flaws can you detect in the theory, then?"

"Oh, several, at first glance. Why, for example, was there no blood found anywhere, either on the lines or in the trains?"

"Ah, that certainly is singular," I conceded. "The report of internal bleeding seems absurd when coupled with the evidence that youth's collars and jacket were soaked in blood. Surely his clothes alone cannot have prevented all the blood from dripping onto the ground."

"Precisely, my good Watson; even my comparatively limited medical knowledge tells me that when a human head receives so massive a blow as Cadbury is reported to have received—his head was fairly smashed open by all accounts—some shedding of blood at least is to be expected in the immediate vicinity. No, no, he bled profusely when he died, I am sure, only there was no blood found inside a carriage, because he was never inside the train at all."

"What?" I cried. "Not inside a train? Where, then?"

"My idea is that the body was lying on the roof of the train."

"What?" I cried again, thoroughly surprised. "How, pray, did it get up there?"

"That is what we must find out. But consider, Watson, the angle and the distance between the body's position and the curve of the rails just as it hits upon the switches. A train would shudder as it swings over the switches, but it would not dramatically affect anything inside the train. An object upon the roof, however, would undoubtedly be thrown far off by the combined jostling of the switches and the impetus of the curve."

"That would explain the lack of blood anywhere in the carriages or on the rails," said I. "But Holmes, your theory is..."

"Still only a theory, I know," he said, interrupting me mid-sentence. "It is merely an idea, and I will not swear to it until I have more facts. But as I said, the more I reflect upon the absurdity of the whole thing, the more I am convinced that it must have occurred in that way, and in no other."

"But why was he placed on the roof of a train, of all places, and how was it managed?"

"I have an idea that my sister can help us there. Her answer to my wire may prove to be most enlightening. Not another word about it now, Watson, until we have more data."

My mind raced to explore Holmes' theory, though I confess I failed to see how it could possibly have any bearing on the case; nor could I imagine how a comprehensive list of foreign spies and agents could possibly assist Holmes in any way, unless he already suspected some person or persons, and merely sought confirmation. Though I explored the matter from every conceivable angle, I had come no nearer to guessing Holmes' chain of reasoning by the time we reached Woolwich.

From the station, we proceeded by cab to the house of the late Sir James Valentine. It was a fine villa, with green lawns stretching down to the Thames. The fog had lifted somewhat, and a watery sunshine endeavored to dispel the wisps that still clung to the hedges and hollows. I basked in the evidence of soon-to-come springtime as we walked up the garden path to the house.

The mood relapsed again into sober gloom, however, as a butler in mourning velvet answered our knock, and led the way with stricken step to a dim-lit drawing room, where we were asked to wait. Presently the butler returned and announced Miss Valentine. The lady herself entered, her reddened rims and untidy blonde locks attesting to her sudden double bereavement. Holmes bowed low and presented his card with a flourish.

"My sincerest sympathies, madam," said he. "I deeply regret the necessity to disturb you at this time; however I must prevail upon you to answer a few questions, which may go far in assisting us to clear up the tragic circumstances surrounding your fiancé's death, and that of your worthy brother."

"I shall try, Mr Holmes," said the lady, seating herself upon a settee and motioning for us to do likewise. "Though everything has happened so suddenly; I confess I can scarcely take it all in."

"Perhaps it will be easier if you limit yourself to answering my questions."

"Infinitely so," replied the woman, with a grateful sigh. "Ask me anything you like; I shall try to answer to the best of my ability."

"When did you last see Mr. Cadbury?"

"Last night. We were walking to the theatre—the fog was so thick that a cab was useless—when suddenly he dropped my arm, told me forcefully to go back home, and darted away into the fog. I was startled, but when he did not return after a few minutes, I came back home."

"Extraordinary!" murmured Holmes. "Can you explain his conduct?"

"No, not for the world! We had been conversing most amiably, and nothing at all seemed amiss, until that moment."

"That is most singular," Holmes remarked. "Tell me, Miss Valentine, can you say for certain whether he had any worries—anything on his mind? Was he in want of money, for example?"

"No, his wants were simple, and his salary most adequate. He had saved several hundred, and we were to be married next year. He had had no upsets of late, at least none that he revealed to me."

"Do you know anything about the technical cards found in his pockets?"

"Technical cards? Ah yes, my brother mentioned Engine cards of some sort in his farewell letter to me," she said. "He said that Arthur had stolen cards containing a state secret of great value. I cannot help you in any way there, Mr. Holmes; I really know very little about my brother's work, and less of my fiancé's. Neither of them ever discussed their affairs with me."

"I see," said Holmes. "And what of your brother, Sir James? Can you give us any clues to help us understand the circumstances surrounding his personal tragedy?"

Miss Valentine's pretty face, which had hitherto been composed, though sad, began to work convulsively. She brought her handkerchief to her face and sobbed piteously for a few moments, struggling to regain her composure.

"It... it was this dreadful scandal," she said, between weeping sobs. "He... he couldn't take it, I suppose. His honor was so dear to him, and his pride in his department so profound, that it broke his heart to hear that one of his own trusted men could do such a thing. His letter to me said as much. My own dear, dear brother. Oh, Mr. Holmes, I am desolate, desolate." She trailed off again into a burst of quiet weeping behind her handkerchief. My sympathy flowed towards this beautiful girl, so dreadfully bereaved, so fragile and helpless against the flood of ill-luck which had suddenly drenched her life. She recovered presently, and begged our forgiveness for her outburst.

"Not at all, dear Miss Valentine," I hastened to reassure her. "On the contrary, it is most wretched that we should have to intrude upon your sorrow in this fashion. Mr. Holmes and I shall do everything in our power to discover the truth of the matter, in the hopes that we may speedily bring closure to this tragedy." I threw a glance in Holmes' direction, and saw that his brow was deeply furrowed.

"Yes indeed, Miss Valentine," said he. "Pray, would it be possible to see this note which your brother left you? A mere formality, I assure you, but one which may prove revealing."

Miss Valentine started violently, and stammered, "Why... no. No, I'm sorry. You see, I regret very much that, in my first shock, I … I threw it into the fire. I thought it was a cruel joke, you see, and you can imagine my chagrin at having done so when a few moments later I learned that the note had not been false."

Holmes reached for his hat. "If there is anything we can do for you, Miss Valentine, or if any fresh knowledge or memory relating to the case arises, do not hesitate contact us."

"I thank you from my heart, Mr. Holmes," replied the girl, smiling through a mask of tear stains. "You, too, Doctor. And oh, I must beg you not to forget that dear Arthur—Mr. Cadbury—was a single-minded, chivalrous, patriotic man. He would have cut his right hand off before selling a State secret confided to his keeping. The facts all tell against him, I know, but... oh, his honor was more important to him than anything else in the world. I cannot explain his actions, but I, who knew him better than most, can assure you that there must be some mistake in all this..."

Her voice trailed off, her liquid eyes and trembling lips more eloquently appealing than her stumbling words. Holmes' face reflected deep gravity as he bowed, and we wished her good morning.

A few words with the constable on duty on our way out divulged the bare facts of the master's death. Around six o'clock that morning an urgent message had been taken to Sir James with his tea; he rang not five minutes later for his valet, to whom he entrusted a sealed letter for his sister Miss Valentine, with instructions to have it delivered immediately. Nearly an hour later, at ten minutes past seven, another messenger arrived with a summons for Sir James to appear at the offices of the Ministry; the valet took the message upstairs, and found the door locked. As no answer came to his repeated knocks, the valet fetched the footman and the gardener, and the three forced the door and entered the chamber, where they found Sir James slumped over his desk, cold dead.

The doctor and police were summoned, and the cause of death was determined to have been suicide by poisoning. The letter to Miss Valentine apparently explained his reasons for taking his own life. So much the constable was able to tell us.

    \*   \*   \*

"Now for Madame Cadbury," said my friend briskly as we walked down the path toward the gate. "I say, Watson, did anything strike you about the young lady whose company we have just left?"

"She seemed dazed and heartbroken to me, poor lass."

"Yes, she certainly had the appearance of one lost in grief. But she retained sufficient command of her wits as to avoid speaking the whole truth, and nothing but the truth."

"Holmes!" I cried.

"My dear Watson, I am convinced that she knows much more than she admitted, and what is more, she lied in one or two little points. I wonder now, whether she was not trying to shield someone, most likely her fiancé. Unless..." Holmes caught his words abruptly and lapsed into brooding silence as we hailed a cab and made our way to the house of Cadbury's mother.

I puzzled within myself, trying to recall whether during our interview Miss Valentine had given any sign of purposely endeavoring to withhold information from us. At last, I shook my head over my friend's cold, calculating nature, so devoid of the commonest human empathy for a bereaved soul, as to be able to coolly suspect her of concealing vital information, or even of lying. Holmes' mental powers are undoubtedly some of the greatest I have ever known, but in the realm of ordinary human emotion, I fear he is entirely handicapped.

Our interview with the mother of Arthur Cadbury was a tedious and painful one. The old lady wept profusely, repeating over and over that her boy was neither thief nor traitor to his country. Holmes, who could be most ingratiating with the female sex when he chose, spent long minutes attempting to soothe her, mostly by vociferously agreeing with every statement she uttered, in order that we might gain some useful data. He asked her trivial questions about her son's boyhood and received in reply a torrential discourse on the delightfulness of her late lad's filial disposition. In vain, however, did he attempt to extract any bit of information that might assist us in our investigation. At length, the tearful interview came to a close, and Holmes and I left, exhausted and ruffled in the nerves.

"My word, Holmes," said I, mopping my brow, "if nothing else, we have at least been given bountiful evidence from a creditable source that this fellow Cadbury is the saintliest of all angels currently residing in Heaven's highest quarters. I pray that we shall not be the ones to disprove that woman's illusions, for it seems likely that she will be sorely disappointed."

"Possibly. On the other hand, Watson, though at present the young man seems cast in the blackest shades, I am not quite convinced that he was the base scoundrel he appears to have been. It is just possible that he, being as innocent as the day, was framed as the perpetrator of this wicked deed. "

"Shall we go now to the offices of the Arsenal?" I queried, spying a cab parked at leisure down the street.

"Yes, and by Jove, let us pray that we find no disconsolate women there."

I vigorously nodded my head in agreement.

* * *

Mr. Sidney Johnson met us at the Woolwich Arsenal offices with the respect that my companion's card usually commanded. His wrinkled cheeks were haggard, his face gruff and deeply lined.

"It is deplorable, Mr. Holmes. Our chief dead, Cadbury dead, the cards stolen. The place is thrown into confusion. And yet, yesterday we were as efficient an office as any in the government service. To think that Cadbury—Cadbury! Whom I trusted as I trust myself—could do such a thing."

"You have no doubt that it was he who took the cards?"

"Well..." Mr. Johnson sputtered, surprised at the question, "the cards were found on him, were they not? Who else could have taken them?"

"That is exactly what we are set to find out. Tell me, Mr Johnson, what time was the office closed yesterday?"

"At five. I always stay on after the others leave, and see that all is properly locked up. I personally secured the cards within the strong-room, where they are always kept except when they are in use. This morning I did not notice that anything was amiss, until the police questioned me about my clerk, and we discovered that the cards were missing from the strong-room."

"Quite so," said Holmes. "Tell me, did Cadbury possess, or have access to, keys to the office and strong-room?"

"Only to the office itself. He did not, to my surest knowledge, have a key either to the outer door of the building, or to the strong-room. I have one set, and the other was in Sir James' possession. My set never leaves my watch-chain," Mr. Johnson pulled a ring of keys from his waistcoat pocket as he spoke. "And Sir James was known for his meticulous carefulness in all security matters. His caution was a byword among his employees and associates."

"I see," said Holmes, briefly inspecting the keys in the clerk's upturned palm. "Well, well, if Cadbury is the culprit, must have obtained a duplicate set somehow. And yet none was found upon his body, nor in his rooms. How very singular. One other point: if Cadbury had desired to sell the plans, would it not be far easier simply to copy the plans for himself than to take the originals, as was actually done?"

"It would have been difficult," said Mr Johnson. "The cards are complex and highly technical, and are not easily copied."

"But I suppose either Sir James, or you, or Cadbury had that technical knowledge?"

"No doubt we had, but I beg you won't try to drag me into the matter, Mr. Holmes. What is the use of our speculating in this way when the original plans were actually found on Cadbury?"

"Well, it is certainly singular that he should run the risk of taking originals if he could safely have taken copies, which would have equally served his turn."

"Singular, no doubt—and yet he did so."

"Every inquiry in this case reveals something inexplicable. Now there are three Engine cards still missing. They are, as I understand, the vital ones."

"Yes, although there is a fourth card which may be considered of equal importance to the construction of the main ship; I am surprised that it was not taken along with the others. It graphs out the details and positioning of several double valves with automatic self-adjusting slots which control the flow of seawater into the steam-generator that powers the vessel. Even if the thieves are able to understand how the generator itself works—something which we have not been able to fathom—they could not complete its development without the intricate graphs contained in this other card."

"That is most interesting, Mr Johnson. And now with your permission, I shall stroll about the premises."

Holmes dropped to his knees and inched around the office and along the outer corridor in snail fashion, pausing occasionally for a closer look at a misplaced speck, or trifles of the kind. I followed cautiously in his wake, staying well clear to avoid upsetting his research. At one point he glanced over his shoulder at me, and sent me to inquire of Mr Johnson how many people frequented the office adjacent to the strong-room, and particularly whether there were any female employees or frequent visitors.

I returned speedily with the answer. No, there were no female employees in this building, save the ancient charwoman on Wednesdays and Fridays, and no visitors of any sort, besides the occasional Navy officer or constructor who came to consult the plans. Only Mr Johnson himself, Sir James, and Mr Cadbury ever used the offices on this level; three male secretaries shared a partitioned office down the hallway, and were not permitted to enter the main office quarters. Holmes, without a sign that he had attended a single word, continued inching his way to the front door on his hands and knees. He pushed the door open and nearly collided with Lestrade, who stood poised to enter the building. Holmes sighed impatiently at the interruption and rose to his full height, disregarding his dusty trouser knees.

"Well, well, Mr Holmes," said Lestrade jovially, "hard at work, aren't we? Formed any of those exotic and wild-limbed theories of yours yet?"

"Lamentably, no," said my friend coldly. "Although I have discovered one or two singularities which may reveal fresh facts. Your untimely coming has just interrupted a very promising trail."

"Ah, well, Mr. Holmes, even the best of us must deal with little inconveniences," said Lestrade. "When you've been as long in the profession as some of us have, you'll have gotten used to such things." Holmes' thin lips set in a white line; Lestrade chuckled and proffered a small bundle. "I thought you might like to see the personal effects of Sir James, as well as the artifacts found on Cadbury's person."

Holmes took the bundle and glanced cursorily through it; the only item that briefly arrested his attention was a set of keys on a gilt chain. He returned the lot to Lestrade without ceremony, and then excused himself, crouching low again to examine the threshold and step, and proceeded to disappear around the side of the building, inspecting the muddy snow-clad lawn and footpath closely as he went.

Lestrade glanced at me and shrugged significantly. I said nothing, though I sympathized somewhat with his complete ignorance of Holmes' train of reasoning up to this point. A sudden shout from Holmes brought us running around the corner to where he stood before a window.

"See here, Watson," he said, as I approached, "these shutters do not quite meet. It is possible for a person over 5 feet 8 inches to peer into this office, when the blinds are up. Dear me, what is the good of iron bars on shutters that can be pried apart with a common jemmy?"

Lestrade coughed gently. "No shutters had been tampered with, Mr Holmes; Johnson the head clerk was certain of that."

"All the same, Lestrade, it is at least possible that someone may have peeped through this very crack and seen the thief at work in the strong-room, which happens to be immediately in the line of vision."

"Possible, no doubt," scoffed Lestrade, "but highly unlikely. You're asking me to believe that someone just happened to creep through the fog, unseen by any of the guards, to that very window; at the very time that Cadbury was taking the cards. Well, that's fine. Who was this person then? What was his motive for looking through the window? Where is that person now? Why did he not immediately report to the guards? Facts, Mr. Holmes; give me the concrete facts, and the case is quickly solved. Wild speculations and fanciful theories are all right when sitting in an easy chair, but the harsh reality of crime demands that frivolous fancies must be dispensed with, and only hard facts taken into account. I recommend that thought to you, Mr. Holmes. If you'll excuse me now, gentlemen, I must continue about my business." Holmes watched the inspector's dignified departure with twitching lips, and presently burst into hearty, silent laughter.

"We must give him some credit, Watson; he is meticulous in his pursuit of trivial facts, and though he very seldom draws correct conclusions in any save the most childishly straightforward cases, at least he saves us the trouble of having to gather every scrap of trivia for ourselves. Occasionally he has stumbled upon some vital shred of information, to which he himself attributed little or no importance, but which served to unlock an entire case for me. Yes, our dear Lestrade has his uses now and again. But come, Watson, you shall be wanting your lunch shortly, and as I have seen all there is to see here, and there are one or two matters I should like to attend to, I propose that you and I return to Baker Street by the next train."

Mycroft Holmes' reply to her brother's telegram awaited us in our rooms at Baker Street. Holmes tossed it to me to read aloud while he rummaged about among the jungle of papers that adorned our sitting room for a mislaid stack of varied maps of London. Mycroft's message ran thus:

"There are numerous small fry, but few would handle so great an affair. Possible men to consider are Adolphus Meyer, of 13 Great George Street, Westminster; Louis La Rothiere, Campden Mansions, Notting Hill, and Peter von Oberon, of 19 Caulfield Gardens, Kensington. Latter is reported to have left London for Stockholm this morning."

Holmes, having located his assortment of maps, spread them across the table just as Mrs. Hudson entered with our luncheon.

"My dear Mrs. Hudson, you really are dreadfully in the way," snorted Holmes irritably as our housekeeper, disregarding the state of the table, proceeded to set our places with the experience borne of long years' resignation to her tenant's irregular habits. When at last the table was set and our plates served, Holmes' maps occupied the surfaces of the crockery, and he studied them with great concentration as we ate. His animation grew as his research continued; the color crept into his pale cheeks, and his display of impatience when Mrs Hudson once again upset the arrangement of his papers as she removed our dishes was altogether more human than his habitually dispassionate nature allowed, to my great, though concealed, amusement.

At last, after a quarter-hour's earnest research, Holmes gave forth a triumphant cry, and disappearing into his room, presently emerged in the attire of a professional loafer in a slouch hat and disreputable shoes.

"You shall hear from me before evening, Watson," he said as he pocketed a selection of his precious maps and tossed the remainder out of sight behind the sofa. "If my idea proves to be correct, I shall most definitely want your assistance tonight; it may be that adventures lie before us."

"Certainly," said I, half rising from my chair. "Shall I come with you now?"

"No, no," said Holmes, perceiving my intentions, "I am going on a reconnaissance, and must go alone. There are one or two theories I should like to put to test. Never fear, I shan't do anything serious without my trusted comrade and biographer at my elbow."

# Mycroft Holmes

# Chapter Three

All the long afternoon I waited impatiently, vainly trying to imagine the direction Holmes' chain of reasoning had led him; attempting to discern which fact had struck him as the vital clue upon which his interpretation of the mystery was centered. The promised message from Holmes did not arrive until shortly after nine o'clock, just as I contemplated ringing the bell for my supper.

"Dining at Goldini's, Gloucester Road, Kensington. Come at once. Bring my black Engine trousseau from the bureau drawer, the blood-light from my workbench, my burglar kit, hunting crop, and your revolver. Avoid getting arrested, please. — S.H."

Quite a nice collection for a respectable citizen to carry about, thought I. Holmes' allusion to his burglar kit and Engine trousseau filled me with a palpable sense of foreboding, for with the aid of the former he could break into any building, safe and strong-room made by man, and with that of the latter access whatever information he desired from any Babbage Engine, no matter how advanced or complex its programming. Nevertheless, I obediently filled every pocket of my overcoat with the required equipment, and set out into the dim, fog-draped streets.

When I arrived at Goldini's Restaurant, I was greatly surprised to see Mycroft Holmes seated beside her brother at a small round table in the corner, the surface of which was covered with a number of maps, guidebooks, and cigar ash.

"Ah, Watson," called Holmes. "I hope you have not yet had your supper—no? Excellent, you must join us in a coffee and Curacao. Have you brought my tools?"

"They are scattered about my pockets."

"Marvelous! Try one of the proprietor's cigars; they are less poisonous than one would expect. Dear me, what a lovely night; absolutely ideal for our purpose."

Mycroft Holmes raised her eyebrows very delicately, but said nothing. My misgivings returned in a rush.

"What is your plan, Holmes?" I asked, warily.

"My dear Watson," Holmes lowered his voice to a dramatic pitch, "we are going to commit a felony. How does a round of breaking-and-entering sound to you?"

"Holmes!" I ejaculated, eyes rounded in horror. "You don't mean it!"

"Afraid so," Holmes said, puffing out a huge cloud of blue smoke. "You see, if we are to succeed in learning the truth of this strange matter, and consequently retrieving the lost cards, we must discover how the theft was accomplished, who besides Cadbury was involved in the matter, why he was killed, and why the seven cards replaced in his pocket. After my reconnaissance and research of the afternoon, it is clear that our next step must be to search the premises which I suspect to have been the location of the crime, and learn for ourselves what secrets they may disclose."

"We might get caught," I expostulated. "And then what would become of us? These are dangerous stakes, Holmes."

"For home, health, and beauty, eh, Mycroft?—Martyrs on the altar of our country. But perhaps, Watson, I should give you some indication of my reasoning up to this point. Then, if our obvious path remains unclear to you, I shall condescend to further explain the necessity of what I propose to do tonight."

I frowned, but, lighting my cigar, I leaned back in my chair and listened.

"It must be evident to you, as it is to me, that Cadbury's body was placed on top of a train after he was killed, and so came to rest where it was found. Very good. How was such a feat accomplished, I asked myself. Maybe thrown from a bridge or overpass, or possibly an airship. Or perhaps dropped from the back window of one of the many houses and flats which flank the train line. I did not seriously prefer the latter choice over the others until I received Mycroft's reply to my telegram asking her for the addresses and names of foreign agents in London.

"You are aware, Watson, that my knowledge of the byways and hedges of London is quite minute, and my intimate acquaintance with certain unusual features of our great city has in times past been of some use to me. Well, when I saw the name of Caulfield Gardens, Kensington, listed as the residence of a leading international agent, I recalled that some time ago, while on one of my leisurely rambles, I had noticed that the houses along one side of this quiet lane had their backs so close to the railway, as to practically brush against the sides of the trains as the latter rush on by. Woe be to the passenger who leans out of the window along that stretch of railway. At that very point, too, the trains are often held in suspension for some minutes, due to the presence of switches some way ahead, near Aldgate Station, where two Metropolitan lines cross.

"Anyway, it struck me that anybody residing in one of those houses might quietly and easily dispose of a body in just such a way as I had imagined. When I further discovered that the agent residing at that very address had left London precipitately late last night, I was satisfied that I must be on the right track. Mycroft has heard the full extent of my reasoning, and agrees that Mr Peter von Oberon, employed in Moriarty Industrial as manager of the International Research Department, is most likely the man we are after. And as he has not seen fit to return home since his speedy departure after the events of last night, we might try our luck in searching his unsuspecting house for any useful shred of evidence that might put us on his track."

"Doubtless you are right, Holmes," said I, trying to prevent my admiration from seeping into my stern-set features. "But could not we get a warrant and legalize our search?"

"Tut, man; we have no evidence against the fellow; hardly even a plausible suspicion. Besides, in applying for a warrant we would be compelled to put our incomplete knowledge into the hands of the law, and that would be catastrophic at this stage."

"I still don't like it," said I.

"Neither do I," said Mycroft Holmes suddenly. "But I fear my brother is right, Dr. Watson. There can be no doubt that von Oberon had a confederate in this affair. We can only hope that a search of the house will reveal something to help us unravel these mysteries."

"Exactly," chimed in her brother. "Besides, I promise that I shall do the illegal part. You shall do nothing but keep watch, and hold my lantern. Mycroft, I wish you would come along too."

Miss Holmes began to shake her head vigorously, but stopped abruptly and tilted her head to one side.

"I just will, then," said she after a moment's pause. Holmes appeared pleasantly surprised, and taking her hand kissed it gallantly. "Thank you, Mycroft," said he. "You honor us with your company. It's nearly 11. Shall we be on our way? Watson, you'll have to ride with me, and Mycroft can take the sidecar."

Miss Holmes' eyes narrowed to slits. "If you imagine," said she to Holmes in a soft coo tinged with steel, "that you shall ever convince me to ride on that infernal machine of yours, you are very much mistaken."

"I shall accompany Miss Holmes in a cab," I said hastily, vastly relieved. Holmes looked reproachfully at me, but I diverted my eyes and, taking up my hat, left the restaurant in search of a four-wheeler.

Half an hour later, we had crossed through the gate of number 19 Caulfield Gardens, and become felons in the eyes of the law.

Sherlock Holmes courteously allowed his sister Mycroft to precede him up the porch steps, whilst I endeavored to replace the broken chain upon the gate as noiselessly as was possible in the smoggy gloom. By the time my task was accomplished, Holmes had already managed to beguile one of the locks on the front door, and was rapidly persuading the other to likewise give way. In the hazy darkness I could hear the faint tink-ing of his instruments, as I kept my eyes fixed on the street, and Miss Holmes stood idly by.

I noticed in the distance the glow of a lantern slowly traveling in our direction, even as my ears picked up the leisurely tread of a policeman on his beat.

"Put out your torch, Holmes," I called to my friend in an alarmed whisper, "or our presence will surely be discovered."

At that moment Holmes' work was rewarded with a loud click, and the front door swung open. Mycroft Holmes passed into the house first as her brother held the door for her, and I ducked inside last, quickly shutting the door behind me.

The hall was miserable and bare in the dim light of the lantern, no ornaments or bric-a-brac of note to add any personality to the room. Holmes was already marching briskly up the long, curved staircase, taking the torchlight with him; his sister followed. I looked around the hall, my uneasiness increasing as the fan of light extending from the lantern receded, before squaring my shoulders and following my companions up the stairs, hunting crop in hand. Holmes had insisted, as we made the transfer of the equipment I had brought at his request, that I take his favorite loaded crop, while he pocketed my weapon to keep his own revolver company.

Holmes' brisk voice now shattered the gloom. "Ah, this must be the very place. Observe, Sister Mycroft, if you please, the position of this window over the railway lines below. Now, where is Watson? Ah!" he exclaimed I entered the room, and thereupon turned again to the window without paying any further attention to me. "Yes, I'm sure this is the place. Do hold this lantern for me, Mycroft dear—

yes, indeed, this can only be... by Jove, these are bloodstains, or I'm an ass twice over." Holmes seized the torch from his sister's hand, and fumbled with one or two of its dials.

I remembered that some months before, Holmes had toiled several hours at his workbench over that torch, installing a device to which he had assigned the rather macabre name of 'blood-light'. "It illuminates bloodstains, no matter how old," he had told me, "a vast improvement on that clumsy and altogether unwieldy liquid re-agent to hemoglobin I discovered on the day of our acquaintance." And putting out the lights in the room, he had proceeded to demonstrate his new contraption's ability, by pricking his palm and allowing a drop or two of blood to drip onto the bench. I had been most interested to note the effect of the invisible light upon the blood then.

I could see the same effect now as I looked about the room in which we stood. The windowsill and floor appeared peppered and streaked with iridescent green splotches.

"Aha!" said Holmes triumphantly, "What did I say? Blood—on the window, along the floor, across the passage and most probably down the staircase, too." He shone the light along the trail of gleaming green patches, and followed their trail back down the steps.

"Hallo, hallo! What have we here?" he exclaimed, whipping out his powerful lens and inspecting a barely perceptible smudge on the landing. "A footprint, eh? Now this does simplify matters." He proceeded down the stairs, muttering to himself. Presently he bolted back up the steps, looking like an excited cat in his agitation. "Mr

Cadbury was killed just inside the front door; the porch was swilled down not long after the crime was enacted, but there remains ample evidence that he bled copiously. He was then dragged up the stairs, along the passage, into the room, propped against the window, and pitched over the sill just as a train slowed in its emergence from the tunnel. The evidence is indisputable."

Holmes returned the lantern to Miss Mycroft, and resumed his inspection of the window sill. The latter, beyond her first nod of approval, seemed to lose all interest in her brother's proceedings. She lay the lantern gently on the sill, and wandered around the room, occasionally glancing surreptitiously at her watch; she finally drifted through an open door leading into an adjoining room.

I took her place by Holmes' side and watched him inch his way along the sill with his great magnifying glass. The walls trembled suddenly as a train rumbled through a nearby tunnel, and Holmes' cry of elation pierced plainly through the thunderous roar. "See there, Watson, how the train slackens its speed as it emerges from the tunnel? Now then, it has come to a full halt! Cannot anything be easier than to place a body onto the roof of the carriage not five feet beneath the window? And no one inside the train could possibly suspect its presence!"

I could not stop myself from breaking into an expression of profound admiration. "You have again proved yourself a veritable master, Holmes," I said. "Never have you risen to a greater height than this! How you discovered all this is inconceivable."

Holmes waved away my praise. "Tut, tut, my dear Watson, on the contrary. Once I had observed that the body must have fallen from the roof of a train, the remainder of the affair became necessarily trivial. We had only to discover whether anyone had the means of thus disposing of the body, and what his motives were... "

To my complete astonishment, before Holmes had quite finished his sentence, he had hurled me violently against the far wall, and the successive reports of his revolver eclipsed his warning shout. I heard bullets ricocheting off metal with a deafening ring; a volley of flying discs embedded themselves in the window frame exactly where I had stood only a split second earlier. I recognized the cast of the weapons. Chakram discs—Rajput warriors!

Hardly pausing to wonder what on earth had brought Rajput fighters into Mr. von Oberon's respectable house in Caulfield Gardens, and whence they had suddenly appeared, deployed the cannon embedded in my mechanical arm and fired at another disc-throwing assailant. This latter collapsed instantly under the shock of the cannonade. I jumped to my feet and hurriedly surveyed the situation as I leveled my cannon again to take aim.

Holmes' initial shots with his two revolvers had been deflected by the Rajput's armor; he was engaged now in battle with a fearsome helmeted fighter wielding a short curved dirk in one hand and a Khanda sword in the other. I admit I was momentarily enthralled by the sight of my friend firing relentlessly at his opponent; the bullets at that close range found gaps in the armor, and as I watched, his attacker crumpled to the floor with a horrible gurgling noise.

Holmes cast his revolvers aside; in the torchlight I saw the glint of my friend's steel mitts creeping up over his fists, like the scaly skin of a crocodile, with razors protruding between the knuckles, and thus armed he took his next opponent by surprise, even though the latter wielded a Katar, the dreadful Rajput triple-bladed knife, in each hand. The complex movements and lightning-quick thrusts and parries fascinated me, as though I were watching dancers in a complex choreographed display instead of a desperate battle to the death.

But my inattention to my own danger cost me dearly. Just as Holmes' knee crashed hideously into his opponent's solar plexus, a lily-shaped blade shrieked across the room towards me, narrowly missing my face as I jumped backwards and leveled my cannon at the menace. I fired wildly; the blade crashed into my mechanical arm with a jarring screech, and the rope to which the blade was attached coiled itself madly around my arm and person. Further attempts to fire my cannon proved that the mechanism was hopelessly jammed; the blade protruded from my arm like a monstrous appendage. I struggled against the rope, and managed to free my other hand sufficiently to raise the hunting crop against the fourth assailant who leaped towards me in the wake of his roped blade.

Too late, I saw that he wielded a snaking Aara, and before I had a chance to parry his blow, my stick had crashed against the furthest wall, seized from my hand by the coiling belt-like sword. I jerked back as he swung for another blow; I writhed and the rope fell away from around my waist, freeing my mechanical arm. The curved blade still lodged deeply among the splintered metallic factions of my forearm and built-in cannon, but I thanked my good angels that at least my mechanical arm afforded me a shield-like defense against the razor-edged Aara. The sword cracked like a whip against the metal, and I dodged and crouched against the onslaught as again and again my attacker sent the flexible blade flicking noisily about me.

At last I seized my chance, and the Aara coiled itself about my arm. I jerked my arm back, and my assailant stumbled heavily forward, nearly landing on top of me. In an instant I had wrenched the handle of the Aara from him, and we were locked like wrestlers in a deadly grip. His fingers crept dangerously toward my throat; we thrashed about the room, knocking against furniture, sending whatnots and splinters flying. Bullets flying all about us, we crashed at last against a huge bookcase; the books scattered as the shelves tottered and shook, and finally the bookcase lost its balance altogether. And then my assailant and I found ourselves not only fighting against each other, but pushing against the solid mass of wood bearing relentlessly down upon us.

In that decisive instant, I heard my friend call to his sister, and his words sounded as though spoken through clenched teeth.

"Run, Mycroft—run while you can!"

I looked up and caught sight of Mycroft Holmes in the doorway of the adjoining room, glancing impatiently at her pocketwatch. In her other hand she held a smoking pistol, and I suddenly noticed that the floor about her was strewn with slain intruders. Pocketing her watch, she surveyed the disaster zone into which our surroundings had transformed, and called to her brother with a sigh of exasperation, and rolled her eyes.

"Really, brother Sherlock..." is what I believe she said. My opponent was gaining the upper hand,

and I found myself gasping for breath even as I tightened my own grip on him and struggled against the crushing weight of the bookcase.

Out of the corner of my eye, I saw Mycroft Holmes fumble with the jabot collar at the nape of her neck; In a flash, a fabulous mask shot up over her face from within a fold of her lapels; from a crevice she extracted a sort of miniature hosepipe, and pulled it over her shoulder. The last thing I clearly saw was that she hid her eyes in the sleeve of her other arm, and suddenly a dense cloud of vile acrid steam shot out of the nozzle of the hose she held.

An inexpressibly horrible sensation assaulted my face as the cloud expanded across the room; my lachrymal and mucous glands felt on fire, and my opponent and I broke violently away from each other, desperately seeking relief. The agonizing sensation increased; I lost all consciousness.

I cannot accurately recount what occurred during the time I lay unconscious under the fallen bookshelf. Miss Holmes apparently resuscitated her brother, who had likewise fallen in a gas-induced faint, and when he had revived sufficiently (so he told me later) he saw my form sprawled underneath the bookcase, and despaired that I had died. I admit I was deeply touched by my friend's kindly concern for my well-being.

However, I knew nothing of these things until the touch of something cold and wet on my face roused me. Holmes' spreading grin filled my blurry vision, as he applied a soaked handkerchief to my still-convulsing features.

Shuffling sounds nearby caught my attention as I returned to my senses; I turned my head slightly, surprised to see a number of efficient-looking people scurrying about the apartment, dusting surfaces, taking notes, and performing the usual official duties. A man in a tall hat nearby was kneeling on the floor, performing the familiar ministrations of a doctor upon my late aggressor. Two hefty constables were supporting a limping figure, covered in bandages, out of the room. Among these sedulous souls, I noticed Mycroft Holmes standing in the doorway giving orders to one of the men. How long I had lain unconscious I cannot tell; despite the pounding ache in my temples I felt the necessity to leave this battleground as quickly as possible.

Holmes perceived my attempts to raise myself, and put a steadying arm about my shoulders, gripping my mechanical arm with his other hand. Aided in this fashion I soon found myself on my feet again, swaying and a little unsteady, but alive and vitally unhurt. I noticed that the curving blade had been extracted from my arm; turning to Holmes (who was still fussing about my person) I thanked him for his kind attentions. Holmes' humorous grin disappeared and, resuming his habitual nonchalant composure, he opened his mouth to reply, but whatever he would have said was cut short by a half-growled clearing of Mycroft Holmes' throat; she, too, apparently felt the urgent need to vacate the premises. We turned to follow her out of the room, Holmes still firmly supporting my arm.

He stopped abruptly just as we poised to descend the staircase.

"One moment, if you please, Watson; I forgot the torch." He left me leaning against the balustrade, and I turned my gaze back towards the scene of our latest adventure. The blood-light of Holmes' torch on the window-ledge illuminated what now resembled a slaughterhouse; radiant green splotches leered at me from the floor, the walls, the ceiling, the door, and the window, between the shadows cast by the discreet figures documenting the scene. I shuddered in disgust.

"Ghastly, isn't it?" said I to Holmes when he returned with torch in hand.

"Did you think so?" he replied, with a look of angelic innocence spread across his bruised features. "I'm sure the exercise was most refreshing."

I looked at my friend askance as we limped painfully down the stairs, and I could only shake my head grimly in wonder.

* * *

My cab decanted me not an hour later before our apartments in Baker Street, and I mounted the steps slowly and painfully. I was surprised to see Holmes sitting comfortably by the fire, looking very much recovered from our recent adventures, though the shadows cast on his face by the firelight displayed a mottled disarray of unusual colors, and I noticed that a handkerchief had been clumsily wrapped about one hand in lieu of a proper bandage. Clad in his mouse-colored dressing gown and slippers, with his pipe at its usual angle between his lips, and a small pile of fly-leafs and newspaper cuttings in his lap, he looked the picture of casual comfort and relaxation. He glanced up as I entered, and chuckled at my woebegone appearance.

"My dear Watson," said he, "there is much to be said for a wind-sweeping drive after heavy physical exertion; I feel positively renewed after my short journey, while you stagger in as though you had not slept in days. Your face is an unwholesome shade, man; may I recommend a stout nightcap? Dear me, we must get that arm of yours looked at; if you leave it on the coffee table I shall try to repair it later. You may need it tomorrow."

I obediently poured myself a tumbler of whiskey, and sank into my chair opposite Holmes, while he facetiously proposed that fate must be utterly opposed to the idea that I should possess a right arm, for all its attempts to deprive me of that useful member. I declined to appreciate the humor of the thought, however, and when Holmes' chuckles died down, I gave myself up to mentally cataloging my injuries. Presently, however, I roused myself sufficiently to take notice of my friend's doings. He had risen to fetch his Persian slipper, bulging with tobacco, and a great bundle of newspapers, and had nestled once again in his chair, propping his feet up on the edge of the grate. Blue swirls issuing from his favorite pipe encompassed his thin, ascetic face, and disappeared into the shadowy corners of the ceiling beyond the firelight.

"Holmes!" cried I with a reproving frown. "You are not going to stay up all night, are you?"

"It is necessary, Watson," came the laconic reply. "The case, as you are well aware, hinges on time. If we are sluggish in our attempts to recover the lost technical cards, chances are they shall pass forever out of our reach. We must act quickly, but what must our actions be? I have not stopped for a moment's quiet reflection all day, and once or twice in times past when dealing with timely matters, I have found that a silent night's vigil over an ounce or two of shag can do wonders for the reasoning faculties. I strongly advise you, however, to take to your bed as soon as I have shown you the results of our evening's foray. See what my sister has extracted from among Mr. von Oberon's affairs."

Holmes handed me a few of the papers I had observed him perusing when I had entered.

"Cuttings," said I, looking the leaves over.

"From the agony column in the Daily Telegraph," continued Holmes, coming forward to stand beside my armchair. "They are a sequence of correspondence between two individuals called 'Pierrot' and 'Sieg'. My guess is that these are the assumed names of von Oberon and his accomplice. They order themselves."

I read several aloud.

"'Hoped to hear sooner. Terms agreed to. Acquisition within fortnight. —Sieg.'

"'Matter presses. Discovery imminent. No more letters at present address. Will confirm by advertisement. —Pierrot.'

"'Stinking Wharf, care of same steward for PN. —Pierrot.'

"'Confirm Monday night after nine, residence. Goods in possession by then. Two taps. Leave at once. —Sieg.'"

"A cryptic record, to be sure," said I.

"Indeed," replied Holmes, taking up the papers and receding into the comfortable depths of his armchair. "And yet I feel that there is, at the heart of this broth of mysteries, a very simple solution. We have, I believe, most of the threads in our possession. If, by careful tracing and inspection of these threads, we fail to reach the truth, it shall be entirely our fault. And now Watson, off with that derelict arm of yours, and then I shall say to you, good-night."

# Inspector Lestrade

# Chapter Four

I awoke early the next morning to the sound of a low explosion somewhere very nearby, followed by a dreadful trembling of the walls about me, and the distant tinkling of glasses and crockery. Instantly recalled to my senses by this unheralded blast, reminiscent of my days on the battlefields of Afghanistan, I leaped precipitately from my bed, disregarding the stiff soreness of my battered body, and hastened to discover the source of the explosion.

I reeled upon entering our sitting-room. An acrid smell distinctly familiar to my military nose mingled with the dense clouds of tobacco smoke; my stinging eyes searched the fog for any sign of Holmes, for I greatly feared that, in the course of some ghastly chemical experiment, which it was his frequent habit to perform during his leisure moments, he had at last blown himself to bits.

A heady chuckle met my ears, and I located Holmes at last, crouched not far from the shuttered window, apparently inspecting with enormous amusement a great gaping hole in the wall, blackened all about the edges, through which could be faintly seen the gray sky beyond.

"Holmes!" I shouted furiously. "What on earth is going on? What is the meaning of this outrageous mess?"

Holmes held aloft my mechanical arm in a triumphant gesture, but a loud knock pounded outside our door just as he seemed poised to launch into speech. All expression vanished from his countenance and, hastily pushing a chair against the drafty gap in our wall in an attempt to conceal its presence, he went to the door and opened it.

"Why, good morning, Mrs. Hudson. I trust you had a pleasant night? Excellent! Pray, what can I do for you?"

"Mr. Holmes," said our housekeeper in an agitated voice, her face contorted into a grimace, doubtless at the fouled atmosphere which escaped the open door of our sitting-room, "did you hear that dreadful explosion?"

"I believe I did hear a noise of some sort a few minutes ago," replied Holmes, vaguely. "I imagined that your furnace below had done itself a mischief."

"Nothing of the kind, Mr Holmes! I thought the noise came from this apartment. And what is that dreadful smell?"

Holmes turned his head and looked reprovingly at me. "Your senses are uncommonly sharp, Mrs Hudson. Perhaps my friend Watson and I do smoke a little too much. When will breakfast be ready?"

"As soon as you desire, Mr Holmes," said our landlady, consternation still apparent in her tone.

"Good, good. Watson and I shall want breakfast immediately. I wish you the finest of days, Mrs Hudson."

"Holmes!" exclaimed I when he had shut the door. "What have you been up to?"

"Oh, merely testing a new gadget I installed into the crook of your mechanical arm. The internal cannon was unfortunately destroyed during our fun yesterday, and so rather than attempt to restore it by lengthy pains to its former state, I opted instead to pitch it altogether, and installed in its place that beautiful little rocket-launcher I picked up at the Russian armory."

"What?"

"Oh, didn't I give you any description of the case which took me to Moscow last autumn, Watson? It had some singular features of interest, and its solution depended upon the mysterious disappearance of a certain diamond-studded dog-collar, of immense value. When I had solved the case to the satisfaction of my illustrious patron, I was accorded the honor of a guided visit through the armory, and received as a token gift this fully-functional scale model of a magnificent rocket-launcher of mammoth proportions. You can imagine how pleased I was to have acquired the miniature, and how I regretted not having a proper opportunity in which to test its alleged powers of destruction. Well, I have tested it at last, and you may observe for yourself how pleased it seems to be in its cozy new niche, and what glorious damage it is capable of inflicting upon its opposer, when skillfully handled. I've no doubt she will be to you an admirable companion and worthy comrade in battle."

Holmes demonstrated the various mechanics of the instrument—such as were visible, that is, above the gleaming surface of my newly-repaired arm—as he spoke, and proceeded to fasten the refurbished arm to the attach-plugs and braces set within my shoulder. I tightened the leather cinches which circled my left shoulder and chest, noticing that the weight of my metallic member had diminished significantly now that its heavier impedimenta had been replaced by a much lighter weapon.

"Ah, here is our breakfast. Come, Watson, for in the excitement of my experiment this morning, I clean forgot to tell you of the conclusions I reached last night, as I meditated over shag and our present case. Let us sit down, and after breakfast, I shall recount all, for I am famished after my nocturnal exertions.

     *  *  *

Our breakfast was spread, and I retrieved from the pageboy our daily pile of periodicals. Elsewhere I have described my friend's avidity for the personals and agony columns of most of our London dailies and weeklies. Into our not overly spacious apartment flowed an endless stream of papers, periodicals, journals and tabloids of every sort and description, and the criminal news and agony columns were duly perused, sorted according to value of interest, and carefully stored for future reference in massive bundles and scrapbooks.

If, due to some pressing case absorbing all of his vital energies, Holmes was unable to keep abreast of this daily imposition on his time, I was in no wise permitted to dispose of the cluttering flood, though the papers accumulated knee-deep upon every surface in our rooms; during those times I was instructed to either sort through them myself, according to my knowledge of Holmes' interest, or else to store them in some place where they would be immediately accessible to him whenever he chanced to require them, for they were bastions of fresh resource for his insatiably curious and energetic mind. By faithful study of the same, Holmes kept his fingertips upon the pulse of London's society and criminal strata, and this he did with the devoted fidelity of a family doctor watching over a cherished patient.

It was, therefore, upon this fresh stack of information that the attention of my friend Sherlock Holmes alighted at once. As a result of our skirmish on the previous evening, Holmes' sallow complexion was severely transformed by a rainbow of assorted shades; nevertheless the irrepressible light of adventure gleamed deep and bright in his eyes, as a wounded foxhound that returns to the chase after a short reprieve.

"The very first thing to do, Watson," said he, from deep within the folds of The London Gazette, "is to place an advertisement in the agony column of the Daily Telegraph."

"Indeed?" I queried, settling back in my chair with the paper mentioned upon my knee. "To what end?"

"We know that it has been one of the means of correspondence between von Oberon, alias Pierrot—"

"How do you know that von Oberon is Pierrot?" I interrupted.

"Obviously, my dear Watson," said Holmes with a reproving glance at me over the top of his paper, "Peter von Oberon is more likely to be 'Pierrot' than 'Sieg'. Furthermore, I happen to know the identity of the latter, and it is my intention to unmask and capture this villainous person without unnecessary delay. I shall therefore assume the alias of Pierrot, and insert an advertisement requesting an urgent interview with my confederate."

I poised to agree with my friend, but just as my coffee cup reached my lips, my eyes descried a familiar name in the paper before me.

"Holmes!" cried I with a sputter, nearly upsetting my coffee. "Too late! Look at this!"

Holmes lifted an unperturbed eyebrow, and I read aloud, my voice quivering with the excitement of my discovery:

"'Imminent danger. Tonight after ten. Stinking Wharf. No return. Pierrot.'

"Well, well," said my friend with a philosophical shrug, "it seems our quarry have tried to second-guess us, though this rash move shall prove to be their very downfall, or I'm very much mistaken. I shall wire to Mycroft immediately."

"But Holmes," I expostulated, "this is terrible. What shall we do?"

Holmes looked surprised. "Why Watson," said he, "naturally, unless Providence forbids it, we shall join not one, but both of our friends tonight at ten. If we do not catch them then, it shall be entirely our fault. I've no doubt Mycroft will place her agents carefully; for all her habitual lack of energy, she is at least thorough and cunning when she does undertake a task."

"And where do you propose to find them? Surely even you cannot tell which of the thousands of putrid-smelling wharves along the river merits the title 'Stinking Wharf'."

Holmes' expression froze upon me for a second or two, then he threw his head back and laughed aloud with great merriment; an occurrence which I have only observed at rare intervals, and that only when his current foes had great cause to fear.

"My dear Watson," said he when his mirth had somewhat expired, "you must forgive me. I am delighted, truly delighted, at your deficient knowledge of evil. It is a pleasure to me, who constantly find myself hobnobbing among the lowest dregs of morality, to be associated with a man possessed of such upstanding character, that he is unacquainted with certain knowledge considered elementary to the average criminal."

Holmes, observing my blank incomprehension, grew grave as he continued.

"I happen to know that the 'Stinking Wharf', as it is styled in this short summons, is an unofficial term for the Foul Fish and Fowl club, in east Kent. The nickname is most appropriate, as the club itself is a converted fish warehouse, situated on an old wharf, right on the Thames, between a fetid fish oil refinery and a tumbledown boathouse. A more vile place one could hardly imagine, morally speaking; it is a nesting ground for all manner of wickedness, frequented by blackmailers, foreign spies and local; the unspoken gathering place of the scum of London's high society. You can write me down an ass, Watson, not to have guessed from the first that this club would be our mice's chosen place of rendezvous. I am glad to at last have an opportunity to bring the action of the law into this evil quarter."

I had listened, fascinated, to Holmes' exposition, during which time my eggs and toast grew cold; I reluctantly returned my attention to these now-unpalatable viands while Holmes, who had consumed his breakfast as he talked, snatched up hat and overcoat, and headed toward the door.

"I shall make all the arrangements for this evening, Watson," said he, pausing over the threshold. "See that you are ready for a great deal of action this evening. If you are inclined to be guided by my advice, I would suggest that you dedicate some few moments to testing the new gadgets in your arm—they may perhaps be wanted sometime during the next twenty-four hours. Good-bye!"

The door slammed companionably on my friend's heels.

Some months previously, Holmes, ever on the lookout for adequate places in which to test his dangerous explosive gadgets, had discovered a disused underground tunnel in the vicinity of a noisy underground construction site, and appropriated it as his private target range. I had accompanied him thither on one or two occasions, and it came now to mind as I pondered Holmes' parting suggestion; I resolved to go there after my breakfast and spend an hour or two mastering the mechanics of my new weapons.

Not, however, until our good landlady appeared to clear away the breakfast dishes, did the calamitous result of Holmes' maiden trial with the newly-installed weaponry return to my mind; my conscience constrained me to postpone my plans and devote my energies to repairing the unsightly breach lately added to our already pocked and bullet-marred wall.

Neither my appearance nor that of the wall was much improved when I finally put down my tools at half-past two that afternoon. Surveyed the result of my labors, I admitted to myself that my skills are less suited to repairing crumbling masonry than my fellow human beings; the wall's mien was still one of battle-scarred ill-use, but at least the gaping gash was sealed. Consoling myself with that thought, I brushed away the excess plaster from my hands and trouser knees, put a hasty sandwich into my pocket, and headed out in direction of the tunnel.

* * *

It was close upon seven o'clock when I returned to Baker Street, but I had scarce arrived when Holmes' step was heard upon the stair. He sauntered into the room, tossing hat and coat aside, and collapsed into his chair. There he sat in dreamy-eyed abstraction, humming snatches of a tune, lost in another dimension.

Not wishing to disturb his reverie, I lit my pipe and sat in my own chair, opposite the fire, and rested my feet atop the grate. The air was chilly that evening, for Spring had not yet peeped out amid the droplets of melting snow, and though the Winter had not been a particularly cold one, my afternoon's exertions in a clammy underground tunnel with makeshift practice targets, and my long tramp home in the damp, smoggy dusk, had awakened in me the desire for warmer weather and fresh life among the stems and branches. Engaged in these thoughts, while the smoke curled pleasantly about my ears, I was disturbed by a vigorous resurgence of Holmes' humming, his fingers tapping noisily in beat to music conjured by his memory.

"I have been to see Brahms' Rinaldo this afternoon, Watson," said he presently. "There is nothing so soothing and yet invigorating as a good cantata. Music refreshes the mind without detracting energy from the vital sources so elementary to the unraveling of mental complexities. We have much yet to discover, Watson, in this little problem so kindly extended to us by sister Mycroft; yet I believe that we are on the right track. There is, I think, much, much more beneath the surface of the plot than is apparently revealed in the bold features of this case."

I pondered this statement while I tapped out my pipe ashes; hearing a throaty chuckle, I glanced up and observed Holmes' eyes alight with sardonic merriment, gazing at the glaring patch of uneven plaster which, rendered conspicuous in the gas-lit ambiance, marked my morning's attempts at masonry.

"You employed your time very kindly today, Watson," said Holmes, still chuckling. "Although I cannot tell whether the good Mrs. Hudson will prefer your treatment of the poor wall to my own. "

"Holmes!" said I, an acrimonious tirade on the subject of his dreadful recklessness and slovenly habits rising up in my throat. But Holmes' expression of abject contrition checked my reproaches, though his eyes still twinkled with a roguish merriment, and I retreated into silence with a shake of my head.

Holmes suddenly shook off his lethargy and catapulted out of his chair.

"It is nearly seven-thirty," said he, "and Mycroft is expecting us at a quarter to ten. If you'll ring for our supper, I shall gather one or two things which I fancy may come in useful tonight."

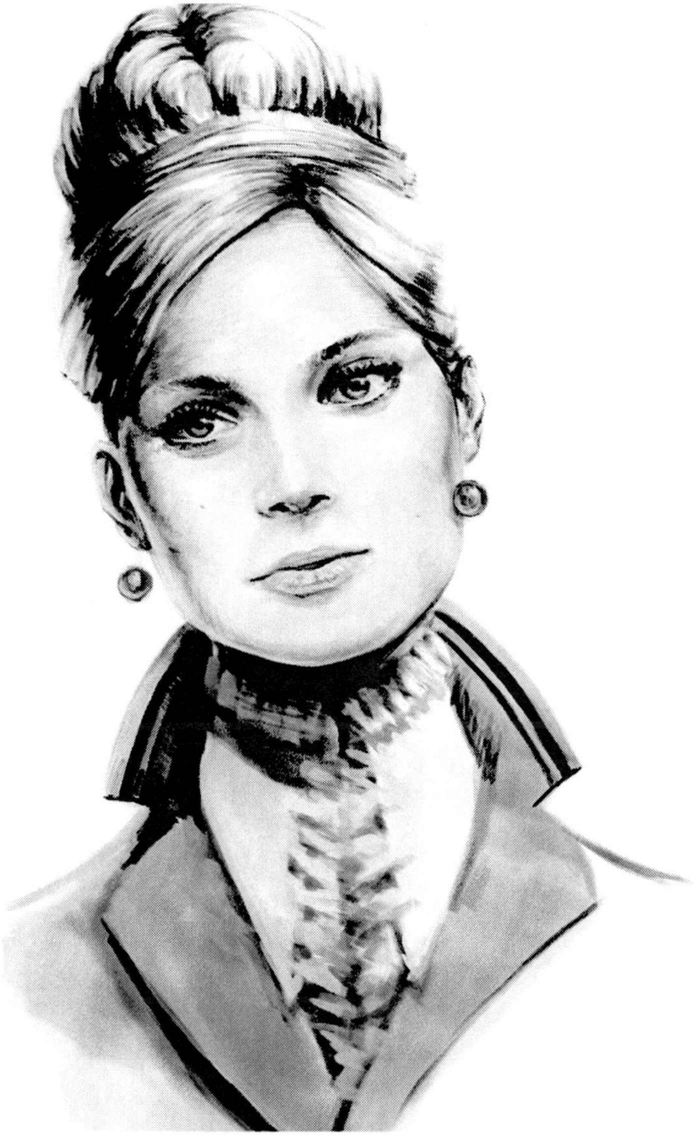

# Victoria Valentine

# Chapter Five

Our ride through the darkened streets of London was rather a long one, fraught with all the customary dangers occasioned by Holmes' seemingly maniacal aversion to caution in his driving. Arriving in east Kent without mishap, we wended through tumbledown alleys and dark streets lined with deserted warehouses, in the direction of the river.

Presently Holmes slowed the Widowmak'r, and switched off the first stage of the motor, until the sound of the powerful twin cylinders died down, and we continued on in near silence, crawling to a halt at last in an alley as unwholesome as it was dark. A shadowy figure emerged and accosted the Widowmak'r on Holmes' side. I stiffened and braced myself in case of an attack, but Holmes, not in the least alarmed, dismounted and motioned to me to do likewise.

"Ah, I'm glad to see you here, Jojo," Holmes said to the newcomer, and then turned to me. "Watson, this is Mr Jojo Pykools, one of my most trusted irregulars. There are few finer motor-drivers in all of London."

When I had extricated myself, Holmes whispered, "Wait here one moment, Watson, I shan't be long." And, accompanied by the slight fellow who had met us upon our arrival, he guided the Widow into an unlit shed across the narrow alley.

I waited in silence for Holmes' return, stamping my feet against the damp chill, while the particularly foul pong in the air, like that of stale grease mingled with mold and rotten fish, made my nostrils curl in disgust. Holmes emerged presently and, taking my elbow, led me back down the alley, around the corner of a wooden building which appeared to be in the last stages of decay, and came to a stop before a nondescript door set in a squat brick building. Holmes knocked briskly with his cane.

The door opened, letting out a gush of harsh yellow light over the gray and black stones at our feet, and a surly keeper peered around the door suspiciously. He looked my companion and me up and down, and relented at last with a reluctant,

"Evening, Cap'n Basil, sir."

"An' good-evening to you, too, my good man," replied Holmes briskly in a guttural twang, exhibiting no surprise at the man's address. "Might I beg a table for my friend and myself? I assure you we would be no end grateful to exchange the raw damp of this evening for a few pints of your choice bitter."

"Right, Cap'n, sir; this way, then." The massive fellow bowed in a grotesque attempt at ceremoniousness, and shut out the cold air to our backs. While he was thus employed, I turned towards my companion, and suppressed with some difficulty an exclamation of surprise. For in the gas-lit passageway Holmes was utterly unrecognizable as the lean, ascetic consulting detective I knew so well. Indeed, his appearance was so altered, I believe I might have passed him by on the street without knowing him. It was not so much his actual features that were changed, except that he wore a captain's bonnet, a patch slung over one eye, and the neckerchief and collar of a sailor's pea jacket peeped out from his overcoat; his entire manner and bearing had become that of a stern, hardy young sea-captain, confident in his command, lacking neither in courage nor audacity. A pair of shining scuffs completed his nautical outfit to perfection.

Holmes smiled at the astonishment in my eyes, as we followed our guide along a narrow passage of worm-eaten floor planking, and down a disreputable flight of steps. Thus, 'Cap'n Basil' and I entered the subterranean den of mischief known as the Foul Fish and Fowl Club.

*  *  *

It was a sprawling chamber of enormous dimensions into which we entered, riven at intervals with chest-high walls lined with rich velvet, which served to create an illusion of privacy for the occupants of the tables along the walls. The ceiling was enshrouded in deepest gloom, far beyond the reach of the gas lamps, which, though numerously scattered about the premises, all seemed to have their shutters drawn half-way, so that the atmosphere was dim, and hazy with smoke. My companion led the way down the few steps into the main room, and strolled in a rolling gait towards an untenanted table in a couched and half-curtained recess.

Not wishing to address my companion until he should have occasion to brief me, I sat down nervously, looking about with as nonchalant an air as I could muster, while Holmes settled his coat and mine on a convenient hook in the corner of our recess, and signed for drinks.

When he had settled himself across the table, I ventured a quiet remark.

"Captain Basil, eh? You've been here often, I gather?"

His eye twinkled. "More than once. As I say, the home-brew is particularly fine." Lowering his voice to the faintest whisper, he said, "We await Mycroft's cue." Aloud again, he cried, "Ah, here are our drinks! Long life an' health to you, m' dear Finch, and may your tenure here be prosperous!" Following his lead I drained my cup; Holmes sighed contentedly and flicked his fingers for another round. The strong bitter seared my throat pleasantly, and I agreed that the brew of the establishment was decidedly good.

While we waited for another drink, I looked about, wondering when Mycroft would make her appearance, for it was twenty minutes past ten already. My field of vision was somewhat limited by the boundaries of our recess, and the few tables within my sight were mostly untenanted, while some were occupied by individuals or pairs. I speculated whether any of these might prove to be our quarry. Holmes appeared to be thoroughly engrossed his second drink, paying no attention whatsoever to our surroundings. His behavior surprised me, for I had imagined that he would be watchful, intensely on his guard, with every sense acutely tuned in to the scenery about us; how else could he manage to identify and ensnare his prey?

Presently a lady, rather short of stature and wearing a dark veil over her features, passed by our table and disappeared beyond my range of vision. She was followed a moment later by a very tall woman dressed in deep purple and black, with a detail of black lace around the eyes, and a sweeping train of the most remarkably exquisite black fur. Though she did not so much as glance in our direction as she passed us by, I recognized her instantly, and my heart, I am forced to admit, skipped a beat or two in appreciation of her elegance and beauty.

Holmes, giving no sign of having noticed either lady, quaffed his third cup with a flick of his wrist, and stood up. "Come along, Finch," said he in the character of Captain Basil, flinging my coat across to me. I quickly drained my own glass, and donned my coat. My companion, swinging his stick jauntily, tossed a handful of coppers onto the table, and in his brisk seamanly step, strode around the partition that divided us from our neighbors behind my bench. Stopping before the table, he removed his hat and extended his hand to the gentleman who occupied the place.

"Evening to you, Mr. von Oberon," said Holmes in his own, ironical voice. "Or shall I call you Pierrot? Mind if my friend and I take a seat at your table?"

The gentleman's eyes rounded, and he stared at Holmes with an expression of mingled surprise and consternation.

"I beg your pardon, sirs," said he in a reproachful voice. "I am afraid I have no idea what you mean. And, agreeable though your company might be on any other occasion, my friends, my lady has only stepped away for a moment, and will doubtless take exception to finding you in her place when she returns."

"Oh, you needn't fear for Miss Valentine; I assure you she is in good hands. The best, really, considering..."

My friend's voice trailed off at the change in the gentleman's expression. He was a dark man, not more than five-and-twenty, with handsome, well-cut features, wide-set eyes, and a peculiar rich tint to the skin; his face, however, had assumed a rigid and chalky quality at Holmes' last statement, his formidable black eyes widened, and his lips compressed in an attempt to regain his composure. This he did, by degrees, as Holmes removed his coat and hat and placidly sat down opposite him.

"This is absurd," said the gentleman, with darkening brow. "I must insist that you desist this unmannerly conduct and leave my presence at once."

"That is, I am afraid, quite impossible just at present, Mr. von Oberon," Holmes replied with a little smile. "You see, I very much wished to have a private word with you. I'm not sure you know who I am, but I assure you that if you deal squarely and openly with me, you may find me a less noisome burden than the appointed guardians of the law, which are your only alternative. Then again, why should you trust me, a perfect stranger? You may take my word, Mr. von Oberon, that unless you take me entirely into your confidence and make a clean breast of everything, your fair companion may be held to blame for matters which, one might suppose, do not concern her in the least."

"Never!" cried von Oberon, leaping to his feet and glaring at Holmes with a fury that did nothing to move my friend, though I reached instinctively toward the brace of my cannon. Remembering in time the modifications that had been done to my arm's weaponry, I instead felt for my trusty service revolver, which I had slipped into my pocket before leaving the house.

"Come, come, Mr von Oberon," said Holmes in his most soothing tone. "You really mustn't excite yourself. Let me tell you again that your best and safest choice lies in taking me into your confidence without delay. That's right. Sit down and compose yourself, or you'll do yourself a mischief."

The man, still glaring into Holmes' eyes, sat down slowly.

"Who are you?" he asked softly. "And where is Victoria?"

"My name," said my companion, "is Sherlock Holmes. Miss Valentine is, at present, in the company of my sister. I assure you that Mycroft is an excellent companion, and Miss Valentine will come to no undue harm while in her custody. The young lady was merely detained a few moments in order to answer some questions relating to several small matters in which she has entangled herself of late, including the deaths of her brother and fiancé, and the robbery of some rather important Engine cards belonging to her brother's department. That is all."

"But that is the sheerest nonsense!"

"Come now, my dear sir, come. It simply won't do, you know. We are not children." Holmes' piercing gaze did not flinch. Mr. von Oberon's countenance fell slightly.

"Sir, regardless of what you believe or imagine of my fiancée, will you give me your solemn word of honor that no harm shall befall her?"

"Barring an act of Providence or fate, I give you my word that no undue harm shall come upon her."

"I, too, am a man of honor, Mr. Holmes," said von Oberon. "I cannot allow Miss Valentine to bear the weight of my actions, for she is a sensitive soul, and wholly innocent of any crime. Your reputation has reached even my ears; you are known for your ingeniousness, but also for your equity. If my confession can dispel the suspicions that surround her, I shall most willingly tell you all you wish to know."

"Excellent!" said Holmes. "I must ask you to begin by explaining the murder of Arthur Cadbury."

"An accident—sheer accident, and one most regrettable."

"Indeed? And was it an accident that his body was thrown from your upper window onto a train?"

The man before us drew himself very upright in his seat. It was plain that he was shaken by Holmes' knowledge of his affairs; nevertheless there was something noble and commanding in his posture.

"Mr. Holmes, perhaps it would be simpler for me to commence by relating my background and history; you will find my actions and motives easier to understand once all of the facts are known to you."

"Ah, that would be most instructive. You have my keenest attention."

"You may judge me to be a thief and a murderer, a mere criminal, but I am none of these," began von Oberon, choosing his words with the care of one relating a historical drama. "Though I am known as Peter von Oberon, my true name is Pierre Nemo, son of Captain Nemo, who was once Prince Dakkar of Northern India. Many years ago, in the period that immediately followed the Great Mutiny, he was robbed of his rightful heritage by agents of a cruel and dominating nation, and separated from his loving family. Believing that we had been killed, he swore vengeance, and renounced the world to build his own legacy, in the form of a marvelous submarine, which he named the Nautilus. He was a brilliant inventor, an explorer and scientist, and above all, a man of honor and justice, full of compassion for the weak and under-trodden. His Nautilus became not only a tool for research and exploration, but also a weapon against the proud and greedy, for he maintained that

84

while corruption and iniquity subjugated the earth and the sky, the foulness of Man could never permeate the depths of the sea, where alone could be found true freedom. As Captain Nemo he traversed the oceans, incurring the reverence of some, and the hatred of many. When he died, we laid him to rest in the heart of his Nautilus, and scuttled her in an undersea forest which my father had cherished as the most beautiful place on earth to him.

"I was a youth when he died, yet I grew to manhood under the shadow of his influence and legacy. Several years ago I went to Berlin to study scientific engineering, having assumed my mother's maiden name, for her people had been of German extraction. While there, I learned one day that my father's last resting place had been desecrated and destroyed, and the secrets of the Nautilus stolen by the very nation that had denied him his birthright and divided our family.

"I was justly infuriated, Mr Holmes, and pledged to retrieve the secrets of my father's legacy at all costs, and rebuild the submarine myself. I had his fortune at my disposal, but it was only after long and arduous research that I traced the thieves, and discovered where the plans were secreted. You may well imagine my surprise and chagrin when I discovered that the man who had overseen and executed the so-called salvage mission for the British Navy was none other than the brother of Miss Valentine."

"You knew her already, then?" Holmes asked.

"Indeed, sir, I did, for she attended a Young Ladies' Academy in Berlin, and we had often met at lectures and concerts. We had long been friends."

"Not only friends," said Holmes, narrowing his eyes. "You were engaged by that time, were you not?"

"I don't see how you could have known, Mr Holmes," said our interlocutor, a flush extending over his swarthy face. "I suppose it is no use denying that we became engaged in secret some time before."

"Why in secret?" queried Holmes. "Surely you had no reason at the time to conceal your feelings for one another?"

"Victoria was a vivacious girl, very full of life, and very young. She loved me, but did not want to marry so soon, and desired that our engagement be kept a secret in order to avoid the society conventions imposed upon a woman who is engaged. For my part, I was content with her promise, and did not wish to hamper her high spirits with a premature public pledge."

"I see. Pray continue your most interesting narrative."

"You can understand my confusion at that time, Mr Holmes. I knew not whether she had any part in her brother's affairs, or even any knowledge of them; how could I trust this girl, who was so dear to me and yet so near a relation to one who must needs become my sworn foe? Such thoughts were utterly unworthy of her, I knew, but in my distress, my heart was torn between my love and my doubts. Even if she knew nothing of her brother's doings, how could I exact revenge upon one of her own kin, and yet retain her love? I struggled for a long while, though I attempted to conceal my thoughts from her.

"She is an intuitive soul, however, and having guessed that something troubled me deeply, she begged me to confide in her. At last I yielded to her insistence, and told her all that I had discovered. Then it was, Mr Holmes, that I regretted my previous mistrust. So sympathetic was she, and so moved in heart over the calamity that had befallen my family, at the hand of her brother, that she swore to assist me in any way she could to right the wrong that had been done me, even if it meant renouncing her own flesh and blood. Ah, words cannot describe the great load that was lifted from my spirit when I beheld her pain on my behalf. We were glad then that we had never openly associated ourselves with one another, as that gave us greater freedom to work together unhindered.

"As soon as her term at the Ladies' Academy ended, she returned to England, and set about trying to discover how the plans might be recovered. Her brother was most reticent and protective about his work, and never allowed her into his confidence, though she exerted all her womanly and sisterly influence to gain any information which might assist us in our plans.

"There was, however, a young man in the employ of her brother, who assiduously courted her whenever they chanced to meet. So dedicated was Victoria to my cause, she condescended, at great cost to her pride and even our future happiness, to become engaged to this man, Cadbury, for she believed it to be the surest way of getting at the Engine cards which contained the Nautilus' plans. Her loyalty, self-sacrifice, and pure nobility of character endeared her to me all the more; I have no doubt she would have seen through the marriage to the fellow, and stayed true to him—though she did not love him in the least—if it had been necessary in order to help me regain my lost heritage. A finer woman never walked the earth, Mr. Holmes."

"Pray go on. We know that you kept in touch with each other by advertisement in The Daily Telegraph. Why?"

"At first we wrote letters. But Cadbury was of a suspicious, jealous nature, and kept a watch on her every move, often by bribing her servants, who, it appeared were in the habit of searching through her things and reading her mail. As she lived in her brother's house, her position was doubly compromised, and should our connection be discovered and my identity revealed, it could only have meant disaster. Therefore—for I had by this time taken up residence in London—we decided to use the personal column of The Daily Telegraph to keep in touch."

"And you scheduled your coup for Monday night."

"We did."

"I believe I can tell you what happened then," said Holmes, leaning back in his chair and half-closing his eyes. "Do check me if I am in error upon any point. Miss Valentine broke into the Arsenal Office at around eight o'clock, having first provided herself with copies of her brother's keys, which by taking a wax impression was easily done. Having purloined the cards, she proceeded to your house in Kensington, as planned, never dreaming that she had been followed.

"Arthur Cadbury, who happened to walk by the Offices on his way to his tryst with Miss Valentine, observed--for there is a significant crack between the shutters--that a light had been lit within the office. Instantly suspicious, but not wishing to unduly alarm the guards unnecessarily—for it might have been the chief at work—he crept through the yew hedge, and peering through this breach, spotted Miss Valentine inside. Instead of confronting her immediately, he decided to follow her and discover where she was taking the cards. He proceeded to dog her from a distance, arriving at last at your house in Kensington, where he observed her meeting with you. A violent scene ensued, during the course of which Arthur Cadbury met his death, very likely by accident and not by premeditated design.

"Faced with the disagreeable necessity of disposing of his corpse, you opted to place it atop one of the trains which, by happy coincidence, pass not five feet below your window. A man of your physique and length of arm should have found it no great exertion. Another stroke of genius, which might have fooled nearly anyone, was the idea of slipping the Engine cards of lesser importance into the dead man's pocket, and so giving rise to the assumption that he had stolen the cards himself, and met his end while attempting to dispose of them. Using your personal Babbage Engine, you were able to first ascertain which of the cards contained the most vital plans."

The set face and steady gaze of Pierre Nemo told us that Holmes' deductions had not missed their mark. Holmes continued after a brief pause.

"From your last messages, I gather that Miss Valentine was to have immediately gone away with you, having obtained the cards. Shocked, however, at the grisly death of her alleged fiancé, for whom she may have had a modicum of sympathy—even the best of women are often susceptible in that respect, you know— she judged herself too upset to fly, and begged a few days' grace, in order that she should not be suspected as his murderess. Quite sensible, too; if she had happened to disappear on the same night as Cadbury's death, a search for her would have been instituted at once, tongues would have doubtless wagged in profusion, and her honor might have been forfeited. As she did not wish to immediately sever all ties with family and country, she returned home, and pretended that her fiancé had run away suddenly, leaving her stranded in the fog. An unlikely story, and yet by its own unusualness difficult to disbelieve.

"By the way, why did Miss Valentine steal the cards on the very evening in which she was supposed to have accompanied Cadbury to the theater?"

"It was meant as a blind," replied Nemo quietly. "How could we suspect that his way would bring him past the Offices where he worked?"

"And wouldn't Miss Valentine have been framed for the crime of theft? Surely her brother would have suspected her if she and the cards disappeared on the same night."

"That had to be risked. I could not bear to go away and leave Victoria behind, even for a moment. We are anxious to be married among my own people, and Victoria was quite sure that, even if her brother suspected that she had taken the cards, he would keep her secret to avoid soiling the family's honor."

"Ah, we proceed to another festering mystery. What light can you shed upon the mysterious and sudden death of Sir James Valentine yesterday morning?"

"None, except what Victoria told me of his letter. He did not give her much detail, but he intimated that one of his department had made off with their most valuable information, and as he was himself head of the department, ultimately accountable for the loss, he could not bear to live with himself, and did not wish to stain his sister's presence with his own disgrace. It was a severe blow to her, poor darling; for she loved him despite his reprehensible actions. I gather that he had always been a good and kind brother to her."

"Yes, so it appears, by all accounts. And yet, considering this man's character, it seems odd, does it not, that he should elicit suicide rather than immediately counter the disgrace by actively searching for the lost cards."

"Who can know the inner workings of the heart, Mr. Holmes? Perhaps this man had secret sorrows, which, added to this recent calamity, he found he could not bear. Who can say? For myself, I had no wish to harm the man; I was content to retrieve the legacy that my father had left to me, for I alone am entitled to it. I would not have lifted a hand against him who would soon have been my near kinsman."

"Well, well, let it be as you say for the present. For my part, I shall not let the matter drop until I have learned the truth. One last question, Mr. Nemo, if I may. How came a gang of fierce Rajput warriors to intercept us at your house last night?"

"To answer your question, I must relate some details of my family's history. As I told you, my father was of a noble house in India. When he was driven from his ancestral lands, he attempted to find closure in his studies of the sciences, and to this end allied himself with an eminently erudite acquaintance of his, who, I may say, even now cherishes my father's memory with the greatest respect, and who has honored me with his guardianship. It was from this kind friend that I learned many details of my father's life during that period, for the burden of the past weighed very heavily on my father's soul, and he scarcely spoke to me at all of what he called his broken years. From what I was able to learn, my father found that even his friend's kindnesses to him could not efface the growing rage in his soul against the evils of humanity. He severed his ties, and, taking with him men who, equally disgusted with the despotism and tyranny of Man, had placed themselves under his leadership, he sought refuge and solace in the only place where Man's dominion had never prevailed. Having built the Nautilus in secret, he and his men abandoned the dry earth and resigned themselves to a purely nautical and submarine existence. There were, however, among my father's former retainers a band of warriors, of the ancient order of Rajputs, who, though allied in heart to my father, could not bear to part with their sacred traditions, and chose to remain on land. The Rajputs are a fiercely secretive clan, and they were Captain Nemo's only link with the inhabited world while he was at unmitigated enmity with it.

"When many years later my father found, among a group of shipwrecked survivors whom he had rescued, the wife and child he had lost so many years before, he reconciled with terra firma so far as to anchor the Nautilus in the bay of the uninhabited island which became our home. The Rajputs, learning of my father's good fortune, came to our island and made their abode with us, pledging never again to detach themselves from my family's side. I was made apprentice to their ancient arts, for it was my father's wish, and while I excelled under their tutelage, they became not only my instructors, but my boon companions. They serve me now with the same fierce devotion they tendered my father while he was alive, and I have a company of them at my disposal here, each man of which I count as a personal friend. I deeply grieve the loss of the nine who sought to defend my property last night. Eight were killed, were they not? What has become of the ninth?"

"He is in custody."

"Wounded?"

"Yes, but not mortally so. I do not like to permanently disable my opponents, no matter how fierce, when I have no direct quarrel with them. And now, Mr. Nemo, though your tale is a moving one, I fear that there are conventionalities that must be attended to. The British Navy Arsenal has been bereft of its most cherished secret, and two of its upstanding keepers have been found dead; as our laws stand, I am afraid that you have much to answer for, and that before a proper Court of Law. I am myself a consulting detective, unaligned with the official forces, therefore the matter is not within my hands to judge. I ask you, sir, whether as a gentleman, you will submit your arms and accompany me peaceably, or if you prefer ... well, shall we say, the alternative."

"I say nothing more, nor submit myself, willingly or otherwise," said Nemo, "until I have seen Victoria, and received your pledge that she shall be spared from all prosecution. Surely it is plain that she has suffered enough already, and that she is no criminal. The culpability of any transgression on her part must be laid entirely at my feet."

"I may grant your first request with ease," replied Holmes. "The dismissal of all charges against Miss Valentine, however, must be discussed among other circles. Let me assure you, Mr Nemo, that I will personally see that Justice, in its purest form, is accomplished in this case, for my own honor is at stake. If Miss Valentine is not guilty of any crime, which shall quickly be ascertained or disproved, you have no cause to fear for her."

Holmes, resuming the harsh tones of Captain Basil, bellowed heartily for a garçon, and handed the fellow a slip of paper upon which he had hastily scrawled a line.

"Take this wit' my compliments to the dolly 'oo passed just now; she in the fancy black furs."

"Righ' away, Cap'n," replied the waiter, and turned with a bawdy grin to execute his mission.

Holmes stretched his long legs, and with an attitude of perfect impassiveness and relaxation, pulled out his cigarette case.

"I see that you are a smoking man, Mr Nemo. Pray, help yourself." Holmes lit a cigarette and took to earnestly studying his pocket-watch, while Mr Nemo and I each took a cigarette and smoked in silence. Presently Holmes raised his head.

"Ah, here they come now."

We turned our heads in the direction of Holmes' glance and beheld the tall, elegant figure of Mycroft Holmes, accompanied by the younger lady who had passed by our table some time before, whose now-unveiled features proved unmistakably those of Miss Victoria Valentine. They were as unalike to each other as two women can be, yet equally imbued with feminine grace and beauty of figure and motion; they turned every eye along their path, though neither lady appeared to take any notice of the attention they garnered as they walked the length of the club towards our table.

When they were but a few yards away, Miss Valentine's gentle gaze froze upon my companion, and horror washed her countenance like an

94

equinoctial gale on the deck of a galley. I turned to the object of her vision, and saw, to my surprise, Captain Basil returning her stare, a leering grin spread across his swarthy features.

"'Ello, Vickie," said he in a guttural, mocking tone, lifting, as he spoke, his bogus eye-patch from his left eye, and transforming into the shrewd detective of Baker Street. "So we meet again, poppet."

My jaw dropped in horrified astonishment at this disrespectful sally, so uncharacteristic of Holmes, and most unworthy of his chivalrous nature.

"I beg your pardon, sir!" cried Nemo, springing to his feet. But Miss Valentine's reply was the most startling.

"You!" she shrieked, eyes blazing with fury and horror; she seized a long heavy pin from among the folds of her elaborate headgear, and hurled it at Holmes with all her might.

# Pierre Nemo

# Chapter Six

We gasped in uniform surprise. Victoria Valentine's long stiletto-bladed pin whizzed past us and embedded itself with a thud into the wooden partition which backed Holmes' bench, inches away from his head.

In an instant Mycroft Holmes had seized the girl's wrist, arresting her sudden attempt to fly, and clapped a gun to her head. Pierre Nemo leaped forward with an indignant shout, brandishing a terrible-looking weapon, but Holmes' crop flew up and knocked it from his grasp, which intervention so enraged the man, he seized his own stick and swung heavily at Holmes. I had scarce time to spring to my feet before pandemonium had erupted inside the club. Alerted, no doubt, by Miss Valentine's screams as she struggled against Miss Holmes' restraining grasp, every man was on his feet, every pistol and knife and weapon leveled. Amid the cries and confusion came the report of a gun, and then it seemed every firearm reacted in its turn, and the room was alive with gunshots, men rushing from the shadows, leaping through the curtains, springing madly from every recess, into a chaotic melee.

In my shock I had remained rooted in my place, my mechanical arm poised to attack or defend, when suddenly the scene before me became clear. Mycroft's agents, strategically hidden within the club's many nooks and crevices, or mingled among the guests, had leaped into action at some given signal, and those loyal to Nemo—or, as was equally possible, those scoundrels who tenanted and frequented this barbarous establishment—were responding in like fashion to the sudden aggression. There was a rush of bodies towards the doors, as the more timid, or more compromised, of the clientele attempted to beat a hasty retreat.

A fresh infusion of police whistles and uniformed men scurrying into the great subterranean chamber through various entrances alerted me that not only our own quarry but every other illegal procedure in the club had ample cause for fear that night.

At that moment a large pewter tankard sailed through the air towards me, and I ducked only in time to avoid an intimate acquaintance with it, though I could not wholly avoid a light shower of choice ale as it smashed into the wall behind me. The tankard was followed a second later by a huge hulking form, who in his crashing fall managed to upset our table, one of the benches, and my person; I extricated myself from the scene of collision without any great injury, though the human projectile remained a senseless heap under the mangled furniture.

In the confusion, Holmes was separated from his original opponent, and had barricaded himself behind an overturned table, his revolver spitting murderously at intervals against a gang of ruffians, who, no doubt having recognized the famous detective, had singled him out as their principle enemy. Miss Holmes' appearance was that of a great biped panther, for her black fur train was thrown about her shoulders, and with her face ensconced in the same half-mask that had enveloped her in our last encounter with enemies, she was emptying the charges of two Moriarty-727 pistols into a line of armed roughs, which fast dispersed as some of their number collapsed. Realizing that both Holmes and his sister were otherwise engaged, I scanned our surroundings for the man and woman whom we had originally come to seek.

It appeared that Miss Valentine, having somehow wrenched herself free from Mycroft's grasp, had turned at once to escape; Nemo, on his part, had taken advantage of Holmes' diverted attention to break away from their fight and join his lover in retreat. My eyes, smarting in the smoke-laden atmosphere, quickly caught sight of his tall figure darting through the chamber, picking his way, as it were, across a debris-strewn battlefield peopled with crazed warriors. Not three yards ahead of him, halfway towards the exit, ran Miss Valentine, plainly recognizable by her blonde head, severely disarranged by the absence of the long hairpin which had kept her locks in place. I started forward to follow and arrest their flight, but as I did so, the woman suddenly gave a shriek, and with a paroxysm of motion, collapsed upon the ground.

The man behind her screamed her name in a heart-wrenching cry of anguish and agony I shall never forget. He flung himself down by her side. My training as a battlefield medico sprang instinctively into action. In an instant I had crossed the room, heedless of the flying projectiles all about me, and knelt by the woman's fallen figure. She had been struck down by a great volley of bullets; her blood soaked through her vestures and pooled around her on the ground.

I toiled over the lady in a desperate and futile attempt to save her life. Pierre Nemo knelt opposite me by his lover's prostrate form; he alternately caressed her brow and assisted my actions, as great tears dropped from his face onto the bloody mass of clothing and hair which lay between us. He held her limp hand tightly, kissed her fingers and face profusely, all the while whispering endearments in a language I could not understand, though I thought it might be German.

The shattered body of Victoria Valentine lay heaving, unresponsive to my efforts, until one last long moan of anguish escaped her lips, her eyes became glassy, and the motion of her chest subsided into stillness. Feverishly I cast aside my last reserves, and attempted by every means in my power to bring the breath of life back into the corpse before me. All my efforts were in vain.

I looked up, conceding defeat at last, from the patient who was beyond my reach, to the face of the man before me. His fine, wide-set black eyes, streaming in the profusion of his grief, met mine at that moment, and read in my expression the conclusion of all hope.

His look will haunt me until I too meet my last rest in silence. Never have I witnessed a more poignant baring of another human soul as in that instant, when every vestige of Pierre Nemo's loss and grief was transmitted from his eyes to mine. I could have wept with him, and indeed my own eyes stung with a sudden flux of moisture. We neither of us said a word; for one moment all time was suspended, and the two of us knelt, alone in an empty world of silence, beside the hollow cocoon which had housed the beautiful Victoria Valentine.

Suddenly the moment was broken, the silence shattered, the deafening shouts and noise of gunfire and mayhem once more surged up in my ears and pounded through my brain. Nemo's eyes hardened, rage and hatred welled up, expelling the pathetic grief from his countenance, and he gave a bass cry that chilled the blood in my veins. Then, flinging his lover's corpse across his shoulders, he rose to his feet, and ran through the confusion towards the door.

Sherlock Holmes brushed past me at that moment, running after the fleeing Nemo, a smoking revolver in one hand, as I remained in my posture of genuflection, deeply moved by all that I had just witnessed.

"Been amusing yourself, have you, Watson?" he called to me in passing. "Hurry, man, hurry!" A menacing figure suddenly rose up before him from the shadows, barring his way to the door; Holmes swatted away this obstruction with his loaded crop, and disappeared through the aperture. I followed after Holmes up the rotting steps and along the passageway to the door by which we had first entered.

Outside, the bitter air, tinged with its foul reek, stung our faces after the heat and smoke of the den below. The strife had expanded into the street; police sirens and garish lights pierced through the night mist, illuminating the traffic which jostled in every direction, setting an appropriate backdrop for the bloody battle which raged inside the building and out.

A few policemen, well accoutered in full battle regalia, ran past us through the open door of the Foul Fish and Fowl club whence we had just emerged. Among them I recognized the bulldog countenance and grim-set features of Inspector Lestrade. He did not pause to greet his amateur counterpart, and I admit that neither Holmes nor I spared a thought for the official forces as we swept over the scene in search of our prey.

"There!" Holmes pointed to a figure, dimly visible through the yellow swirling currents seamed with black shadows, in the act of throwing a bulky bundle into a steam gurney some distance away. "There they are!"

I started to run thither, but Holmes' hand stayed me. He pulled a long thin bird whistle out of his cuff and blew it three times; a moment later, just as I despaired that our quarry's getaway vehicle had vanished into the gloom, the rumbling of a powerful motor eclipsed the terrible noise around us, and the Widowmak'r sped around the corner and screeched to a halt before us. I scarcely saw the boy who drove it to Holmes' summons; he seemed to have vanished before ever the Widow came to a full stop. Holmes had instantly leaped astride the seat, and I, without a moment's hesitation, vaulted into the sidecar, and we roared off down the street in the direction of the retreating gurney.

We had not long to drive before we were at their heels, wending furiously along narrow and pitted paths between the dockyards. I saw then that there were at least three vehicles, careening along the streets at a frightful speed. We steadily shortened the distance between us, until we could see the barrels pointed at us from out of the backs of the vehicles we pursued.

A series of bullets sang past my ear; Holmes signaled to me to return their fire. I replied by raising my arm to fire my rocket-launcher. Though lights in the dockyards and alleys were sparse and altogether dim, my target was plainly visible in the powerful beam of light emitted by the compact Ruhmkorrf lamp fixed between the Widowmak'r's handlebars, and presently a dart-sized missile shot forth from its propulsive nest jutting from my arm, just as the Widow swerved around a protrusion in our path. The diminutive rocket traced a wild course and exploded into flame in the side of a sprawling warehouse.

I braced my arm again, took steadier aim, and fired. A burning rush of energy shot up into the flesh of my shoulder as another missile dislodged itself from its constricts and, trailing a glittering emission, crashed into the vehicle before us.

Holmes' lightning reflexes only just saved us from partaking first-hand of the blazing conflagration that had been the steam-gurney in front of us. The Widow sheered wantonly to the left, narrowly abrading the devastated vehicle and its unfortunate occupants, and stormed up a ramp into a boat-builder's shed, through the blackness of which we careened and skidded noisily until Holmes had brought us full-circle, with a few minor collisions along the way, and back down into the street.

During the moments in which we had been diverted from the chase, our prey had turned away from the maze of streets between the docks, and had far outdistanced us across a broken-up grassy plot expanding into the countryside panorama beyond the industrial fisheries, boat-repairers and clustered warehouses on this side of the river. We followed in their trail, Holmes ever unconscious of the colossal bumps and jostles to which he submitted his vehicle's springs, though we did not achieve our former speed.

As we left the dim lights of the dockyards behind us, I became aware of something churning the sky above us as we raced along over the pitted ground, skirting rocks and gullies, after our game. I looked up, and in amazement beheld the ponderous under-gusset of a huge dirigible, its rotors whipping the air like a mighty Aeolus of ancient mythology, illuminated from below by the reddish light of several lanterns at the stern and prow of its cabin. It passed over our heads and preceded the Widow easily enough, though our speed could not have been, at that moment, less than fifty miles per hour, and then, slackening its velocity, the airship hovered close above the vehicles we pursued.

In that whole desolate countryside no lights penetrated the dense darkness all around us, save those emitted by the headlights of the various ground vehicles, and the lanterns attached to the airship. My eyes, however, were not too dim to perceive that a human transfer was being enacted from a gurney to the airship, even as we bumped and jostled our way over the rough knolls at indecent speeds. A long rope ladder, it appeared, had been let down from the flying ship, and by this convenient, if somewhat dangerous, means, a man was endeavoring to climb from certain death or capture into the hallowed freedom of the skies. We were close enough, by that time, to our prey's vehicles, to clearly glimpse the escaping man's face as it came within the glow of the airship's lanterns. It was Pierre Nemo.

When he had vaulted over the side of the elongated cabin, the airship arrested its forward motion, and, performing a perfectly executed about-face, glided over our heads in a south-westerly course. Holmes veered the Widowmak'r around at once in the direction of the city of London, and leaving the remaining occupants of the gurneys to the attention of the agents of the law, whose vehicles I could see racing furiously in the fugitives' tracks with all the velocity they could muster, we resumed our pursuit of the airborne dirigible.

Holmes was compelled to pay closer attention than was his wont to the terrain over which we sped, for the ground was pitted with rocks and deep gashes, and more than once I felt the sickening feeling of weightlessness as we sailed headlong over protrusions in our path, or skidded precariously across ridges lined with brambles. Thankfully, Holmes was an expert cross-country driver, and the Widowmak'r was by no means a machine that required delicate handling. The thought of an upset while driving at high speed in the countryside frightened me far less than the prospect of a violent collision with a team of draft horses pulling pig iron in the heart of a busy London thoroughfare. Nevertheless, as we careened and pitched our way over the uneven ground, I braced my body tightly and committed my health and that of my companion to Heaven's keeping.

As space, matter and time flew past in a billowing, almost shapeless, rush, I despaired that we should ever catch our quarry, nor even approach the airship nearly enough for me to get a decent shot at it; however, its steady course seemed to be affected by a change in the wind currents upon which it had apparently relied hitherto, for we presently found ourselves gaining rapidly on the massive sky-bound vehicle. By this time the Widow was hurtling through the silent streets of some factory town on the outskirts of the Metropolis, which enabled us to greatly increase our speed, but if we had left the dangers of the uneven Kentish countryside behind us, the greater peril yet preceded us in the sky, and every yard we advanced brought us closer within the range of the airship's guns.

An enormous moon broke through the clouds, and by its radiance I saw that the airship's deck was teeming with Rajput warriors, recognizable by their helmets, and armed with the fluted rifle peculiar to their order, which I knew to be capable of firing explosive bullets more than half an inch in diameter. Even now we were being made the targets of these deadly projectiles, and again and again I heard a high sizzling sound rush past my ears, followed by a dull explosion as the bullets made contact with solid resistance. Holmes swerved the Widow about with such animation and violence, I felt as though I were on a ship at high seas in the middle of a hurricane. Willing myself to keep my eyes off the buildings and curbs we skirted so narrowly in our dizzying dance all over the street, I attempted to target the airship with my rocket-launcher; twice my projectiles flew wide of their mark, and as I painstakingly took aim a third time, I heard Holmes' voice shout at me, though I could not hear his words above the wind rushing in my ears.

Holmes suddenly swung his long arm and whacked me soundly on the side of my head. I turned at once in surprised protest; though Holmes' eyes were turned to the road, his finger pointed fiercely at the hood of the sidecar. He shouted again, and this time I understood his words.

"Pull the lever, Watson! Now, now, now!"

I searched for a lever, and found an unfamiliar knob in the sidecar's paneling. I pulled it hard, and to my amazement, a huge Gatling gun emerged from the sidecar's hood. A pair of long-handled levers slid out of matching crannies on either side of my seat, and beckoned me by their very novelty to fondle their gleaming mechanisms. I had had some small experience upon the battlefield with weapons of this sort, but, knowing Holmes' penchant for tinkering with and remodeling the innards of all of his contraptions, I was unsure how the gun would react to my handling.

Fortunately, at speeds of more than 80 miles per hour, on the heels of armed criminals in a magnificent dirigible, I had not much time for hesitation. Twice I heard the clink of metal ricocheting off my mechanical arm, as their massive bullets sang perilously close to their marks, shattering on contact, spraying shrapnel every which way. Fixing my gaze carefully, and bringing the huge gun's firing range within my line of vision, I awaited Holmes cue, and when it came, I braced my fingers around the levers, and set the machinery in motion.

I became dimly conscious of two things as my destructive monster peppered the air before us and our wheels crunched over the irregular debris occasioned by our bullets, and those shot from the Rajput rifles; first, that for all the recoiling effects upon the Widowmak'r and its sidecar, I might have been firing a stationary revolver at 300 rounds a minute, for we lost not a moment of our speed, nor felt even the slightest tremor of whiplash. Secondly, I was aware that it was not by any effort of mine that the whirling gun continued its repeated firing. It fired away merrily by its own volition, until I ascertained that a simple command grip on the left lever served to both halt and commence the process of firing, while the action of the right lever adjusted the direction in which the nose of my weapon pointed

Can I describe the sensations which traversed my being at that moment? We had left the streets lined with darkling factories behind us, and, having strayed from the narrow road, found ourselves once more sailing over hilly pasture-land in pursuit of our target. The countryside, luminous now under the glowing moonlight and reflections of the vehicular lamps, afforded the Widow greater agility of movement. The dirigible before us disappeared briefly from sight behind a low ridge, as we traversed a depressed stretch of ground; Holmes turned the Widow abruptly northward, away from the dirigible's course, and traced a path up a knoll. I glanced around to locate the airship, but our progress took us around a hill which hid the ship completely from my view.

In our long years of association, I have come to trust Holmes' methods, though I admit that for the merest instant I feared that Holmes had finally doomed the chase to failure, and resigned himself to retreat. But my fears were unfounded, for as we reached the summit of the rise, there, hovering over the wide valley before us, was the airship. I saw my target as the Widow screeched to a stop.

Holmes' cry of "FIRE, WATSON!" was drowned as my enormous gun belched murderously from the depths of its revolutions; suddenly the skyline before us was gloriously illuminated with such a display of fireworks as my eyes had never seen.

The hydrogen-filled chambers of the airship's body exploded one by one with a fearsome roar that shook the very air, and then, fragment after fragment of burning material floated or fell to the earth below.

Amidst this glorious display, my heart was wrenched by the cries of the wretched fugitives, trapped in the inferno by the very element that had given them their wings. The screams of terror were indeed horrifying, and I saw more than one man leap to certain death on the uneven plain fifty feet beneath their burning ship. The aircraft, with its gas chambers rapidly consumed by the starving, passionate flames, drifted through the air in a lazy, unguided descent, and foundered at last on the slope of a knoll, a trail of burning debris scattered in its wake.

How long we sat there, watching the fires consume themselves to glowing embers, I cannot tell. By degrees, however, the panorama before us was overrun with the proper agents of law and order, our allies in the chase, who, guided by the sounds and sight of the airship's destruction, had caught up at last—too late—with the quarry we had come to seek.

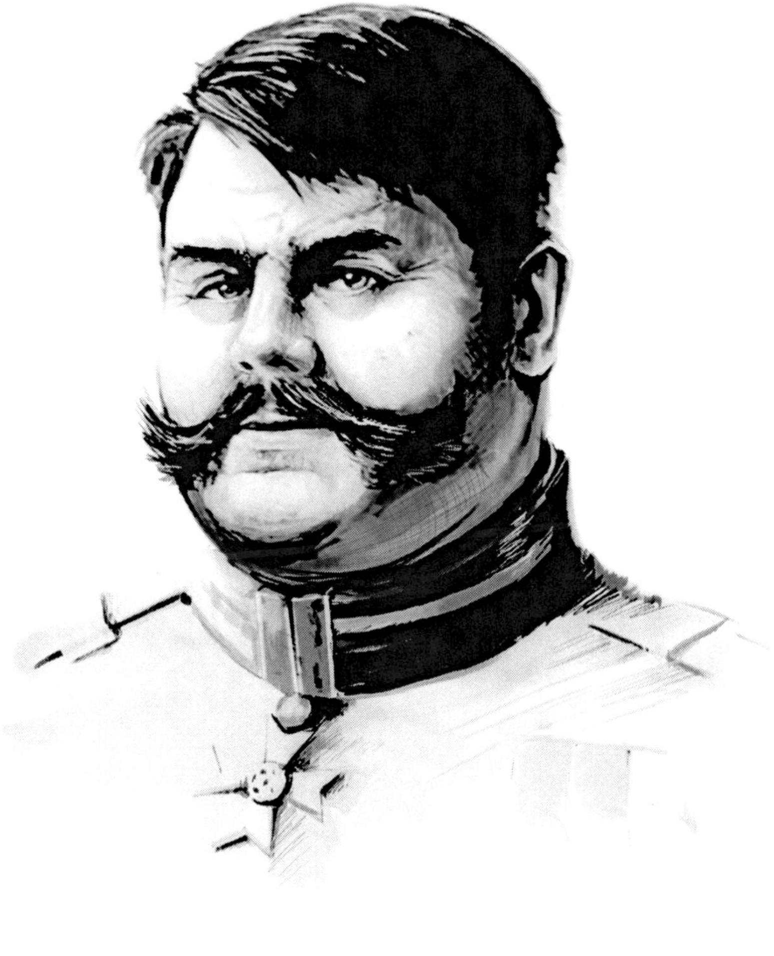

# Captain Valentine

# Chapter Seven

There were no survivors found amid the debris of the terrible accident. Of the twenty-four bodies recovered from the scene, at least three unarmored corpses matched the given proportions of Pierre Nemo, although these were so scorched and charred they could not be definitely identified. Nothing remained of the magnificent dirigible but its badly mangled metal hull and fittings, and of its contents only a few articles of weaponry and other sundry articles had escaped total destruction by the searing heat of the exploding gases.

Holmes and I retired from the scene in the early hours of the morning, when dawn was just beginning to efface the darkness with its fingering tendrils. Mycroft Holmes, pale and weary from the long night's exertions, but ever possessed of her nobility and grace of carriage, met us on the skirt of the hillock. Holmes slowed the Widow and shook her hand warmly. Brother and sister conversed in hushed tones for a moment, and then, with a word and a courteous nod in my direction, Miss Holmes turned and headed back towards a cluster of uniformed men a few dozen yards distant. Holmes said not a word to me during the long ride back home. Even his habitual recklessness seemed to have been satiated for the time being, and we reached our flat in Baker Street without incident or ceremony.

When I awoke later that day, Holmes was nowhere to be found. Mrs Hudson, upon my inquiries, informed me that he had left Baker Street on his noisy motor-bicycle quite early that morning; shortly after we had arrived home, in fact. I wondered where he had gone, and half-expected to receive a message or note of summons. None came, however, and I remained all that day, alone with my thoughts, in our apartments.

The events of the previous night were blurred in my mind into a continuous scene of smoke-ravaged violence and devastation. Our failure to retrieve the fugitives alive—nay, the fact that I had been responsible for the deaths of so many—weighed very heavily upon my soul. The face of Pierre Nemo, when he looked up into my eyes from the body of his cherished lover, haunted my thoughts. Engaged with my morose pensiveness, I lounged indoors for several long, aimless days.

On Sunday evening a dreadful roar engulfed the air, followed by the familiar screeching and thumping sounds of the Widowmak'r's incarceration in the ground-floor garage. I smiled, despite myself. The door flew open, and Holmes came in—I should say he staggered in—and immediately collapsed into his favorite armchair.

"The old reaction is upon me, Watson," said he in a weary voice, by way of greeting. "I shall be as limp as a dust-rag for weeks."

"But Holmes," said I, "what is the matter? Where have you been these past days?"

"Not now, Watson," replied Holmes with a hearty yawn. "I can think of nothing I desire more than to put my feet up, except perhaps to consume something nourishing, for I am famished beyond belief. I have been rather hard on myself these last few days. Has Lestrade come yet?"

"No," I replied.

"Oh well, I'm expecting him here at around nine. I have a bit of news for him, and I thought I may as well tell it him in person as send him a wire. Mycroft ought to be here any minute now too. I arranged to meet both them here at nine o'clock, and it's ten minutes past already. But if my ears mistake not, there is the bell."

It was the Inspector. "Good evening, doctor Watson," said he, shaking himself free of coat, hat and scarf. "Mr. Holmes in yet?"

Holmes himself affirmed his presence in a sleepy voice that issued weakly from the depths of his chair, whither he was curled up, invisible from the door. "Come in, Lestrade. Good of you to come. Pray take a cigar and a seat. Now we have only to await Mycroft's arrival. Oh, that sister of mine! If only she had deigned to accompany me on the Widowmak'r, I might be allowed to take to my bed in half-an-hour. But no, of all the motor-vehicles in London at her disposal, she must needs take the one most nearly related to the snail. Alas! You don't mind waiting, I hope, Lestrade?"

Lestrade's hand paused on its course toward the coal scuttle, where Holmes insisted on keeping his store of cigars, and he looked up with an almost apologetic air on his gloomy face. "Oh, I'm afraid Miss Holmes has had a contretemps of sorts, Mr Holmes; as I was coming here in person, she wished me to inform you that she received a rather urgent summons from somewhere up in the highest quarters, and that she will pop around sometime tomorrow."

"Well," said Holmes, brightening noticeably, "that's something of a consolation all around, wouldn't you say, Lestrade? I think an early bed will do us all worlds of good. How have the investigations been coming along?"

"We've been busy at it, that's for sure," Lestrade said, vainly attempting to stifle a gaping yawn. "We've scoured London from rim to sole, end to end, and not a trace of that Nemo fellow. I'm beginning to wonder whether he isn't really dead after all. For all we know, his might be one of the bodies in stasis at the mortuary."

"Perhaps so, and yet... and yet..." Holmes broke off, and lapsed into pensive silence. "Well, never mind that for now. It doesn't do to brood on matters which are beyond one's control. One can only do one's best, after all, eh Lestrade?"

The worthy fellow agreed with Holmes on that point.

"Oh, by the way, Lestrade," said Holmes, "of course you know that Sir James' death was murder after all, and not suicide."

"Hmm, I suspected as much. Can you prove it, Mr. Holmes?"

"The sleeve of the dressing gown I took away for testing contained definite traces of hydrogen cyanide, of a particularly concentrated solution," Holmes said, rummaging in a stack of odd papers pinned by his pocketknife to the mantelpiece. "A handkerchief impregnated with the solution, held against the respiratory ducts for a very brief moment, would have accomplished the deed beautifully, and was undoubtedly the method employed by the killer in question. Naturally the handkerchief was destroyed almost beyond recognition as such, but I correctly imagined that a drop or two of the poison might have dripped from the handkerchief onto the sleeve. I may add that the empty bottle was found in one of the flowerbeds, complete with damning fingerprints—Where is that blasted paper? Ah!" Having located his objective among the sundry residents of the mantelpiece, Holmes handed a sheet of blotting paper to Lestrade, who read its contents and whistled.

"Well, that certainly backs up your theory, Mr Holmes, to a degree. Where, may I ask, did you get this?"

"Right where I imagined it would be. In the waste-paper basket, chez Sir James' private study. "

Lestrade nodded appreciatively, and said that if there were no objections to his immediate departure, he would be glad for a quiet evening at his own hearth. Holmes agreed wholeheartedly. The inspector shook hands warmly all around, and made for the door.

When Inspector Lestrade had gone, I turned to Holmes, who lay nearly recumbent in his chair, his feet atop the mantelpiece, eyes peacefully closed.

"Who killed Sir James, and why?" I asked eagerly. Holmes half-opened his eyes, and glanced at me with a peevish expression.

"His sister, Victoria." He answered simply.

"No!" I dropped back into my chair, eyes wide with horror and disbelief. "Surely you are mistaken there, Holmes."

"There is no room for error, Watson," said Holmes with a sigh, lowering his feet and straightening his posture, with an air of gravity and resignation to a distasteful task. "As usual, the romantic streak in your character has overridden the evidence of your own eyes and senses. It was obvious that her tale of having received a farewell note from Sir James was the purest fabrication. He did indeed write to her, but it was a demand for instant confession, and not a suicide letter, as she would have us believe."

"But how can you know this, Holmes?" I expostulated. "Surely ..."

"I shall tell you my observations and deductions, Watson. Let us begin by examining the character of the elder brother. Sir James Valentine was an astute man of the world, as well as a brilliant scientist and engineer; meticulous and cautious to a fault, and above all highly protective of what he considered to be his special pet project. I have no doubt that he well knew his young sister's character, and took pains to keep any knowledge of his work out of her reach. He may have mistrusted her encouragement of Cadbury's suit, for it appears that from the time of his sister's engagement, he kept her and her correspondence under constant surveillance. It must be said that Sir James dearly loved his sister and doted on her in every way, but he did not trust her. I'm inclined to believe that Sir James may have hinted as much to Cadbury, for the behavior of the latter towards his fiancée suggests that he was not a man confident in his suit."

"All this is speculation, Holmes," said I reprovingly. "You have not yet stated any real evidence against Miss Valentine, though you cast aspersions upon her character."

"You are right, Watson," said Holmes. "I shall come to that. I had no reason to suppose, during our visit to the Valentine residence, that Miss Valentine was involved in any way in the case. Her statement struck me as singularly flawed, it is true, but I imagined at the time that she might be attempting to shield her brother, or her fiancé, or perhaps both."

"You did mention something to that effect on that occasion," I said, "and yet even now as I recall our interview I fail to recognize an element of falsehood in her words or manner."

"I am not, I admit, the world's greatest expert in psychology, Watson, but the art of being able to recognize a good liar in performance is one which I have devoted some pains to cultivate. I had no idea then which of Miss Valentine's statements were false; I only knew without a trace of doubt that she had not been completely truthful. There is some twitch about the fingertips, some unnatural rigidity or lassitude about the posture and facial muscles, some elusive brightening of the eyes and stirring of the pulse, that transmits 'deception in progress' aloud and plainly to those senses trained to catch the signals.

"The first hint," continued Holmes, "that some woman had been involved in the case came to me whilst inspecting the offices of the Arsenal. You must remember, Watson, that the day preceding the theft had been muggy and damp, with a film of moisture upon every surface in London that was not already smeared with snow. While inspecting the floorboards of the Office and corridor, I distinctly noticed several oddly-shaped impressions, which I suspected to have been made by the heel of a lady's shoe, though by a wide stretch of imagination it might have been the base of a walking stick. Outside the door, however, just before Lestrade made his unwarranted intrusion, I found several very clear imprints of the entire shoe; an arrowhead shape followed by an irregular circle with its northerly rim cut clean off. Obviously a lady's high-heeled pump, and what is more, a lady of small stature, dainty of foot. More tracks of this cast led through the lawn beside the path towards the gate. The fact that the footprints were beside the path and not on it was suggestive. The lady who made those tracks apparently did not wish her steps to be overheard on the gravel path, and so she subjected her shoes and petticoats to the inconveniences of a trek on a muddy border. Fresh tracks they were, too, Watson; and yet upon inquiry, we discovered that the only female who ever entered the Office grounds was the elderly charwoman, whose last visit had been on the previous Friday. Therefore, those footprints could not possibly have been hers."

"Then, too, I discovered other tracks outside the building, pointing to the fact that some man had entered the Office compound through the yew hedge, and stood outside the window with the ill-fitting shutters for some time. The prints I found did not correspond with the cast of boots worn by the night guards; they were pointy-toed patent leathers, of the sort used by gentlemen of modest means on an evening sortie. Arthur Cadbury, as you may recall, was supposed to have taken Miss Valentine to the theater that night. I ordered a plaster impression to be taken of the print in the mud, by the way, and it corresponds exactly with the shoes Cadbury wore that night.

"Inspection of Sir James' possessions revealed that a wax impression had recently been taken of his keys. The set owned by Sidney Johnson, on the other hand, was perfectly clean. This narrowed my range of suspicion yet further, for who but someone very close to Sir James could gain access to his keys, which he apparently guarded with greater attention than any other of his belongings? The evidence I had seen, coupled with the falsehood of Victoria Valentine's story, instantly bonded together to place her in a highly suspicious category in my mind. When later that evening I discovered traces of her presence inside von Oberon's house in Kensington—the very same footmarks as those I had detected in the Offices—I had no further doubt about Miss Valentine's participation in the affair. It only remained for me to probe how deeply she had been involved, and what her exact relationship was to Peter von Oberon. I explored every possible avenue of reasoning, and the conclusions I reached during my wakeful night of meditation were entirely confirmed by the statement given to us by Pierre Nemo himself, with the small exception that Nemo actually had no idea what Miss Valentine's true character really was. She was, in effect, his lover, and had used Cadbury in order to gain information. In Nemo's mind, however, she was not an accomplice, but an innocent, charming and noble young girl, willing to stoop to any depths to ensure the restitution of his rights. He was, to put it plainly, entirely duped by her beguiling ways, poor sap."

"But whatever caused you to believe that Miss Valentine killed her brother?" I persisted.

"Oh, didn't I mention that? It was very simple. When Sir James received the news of the theft at the Arsenal Office early the next morning, he immediately sent for his sister, telling her in his summoning note that she had better be prepared to confess all, or else deal with public exposure and disgrace. He would disown her completely, he wrote, and she would be made to pay the lawful price for her actions if she refused to cooperate. She destroyed the note, of course, and went to her brother's room, prepared, not to confess, but to kill. She knew, you see, that he would carry out his threats. Possibly he had warned her in the past."

"Where is your proof?" I asked warmly.

"In the pocket of Inspector Lestrade."

"What? Do you mean that piece of blotting paper?"

"The very same. It was, as you have probably guessed, the slip that blotted Sir James' actual note to his sister, written in a hasty hand immediately upon hearing of the theft, and thereby proving that he not only suspected Miss Valentine, but that her guilt was a certainty to him."

"The letter indeed proves that Sir James suspected his sister of the theft, Holmes; it does not, however, prove that she did murder him."

"Perhaps not," said Holmes, "unless it were compounded by other evidence. If, for example, your chambermaid testified to having seen you slip furtively out of your brother's room at the exact time in which he was supposed to be committing suicide, and a later search revealed traces of concentrated hydrogen cyanide in the sleeve of the dressing gown you wore when you destroyed your brother's recriminatory letter to you, you too might justly be accused, to use the crude vernacular, of having done him in."

"Hydrogen cyanide?"

"Yes, Watson. One can easily picture the scene. The stern brother, the feigned show of penitence and anguish on the part of the sister, her hysterical rush into her brother's arms, the clenched handkerchief suddenly clasped against his nose—remember that the quick action of the poisonous vapor would scarcely allow time for resistance—the callous expectoration upon the dying man's face, the quick fruitless search for any incriminating documents, the rapid destruction of the little lacy handkerchief in the hearth, and the stealthy exit from the scene of the crime, never noticing the curious eyes of the chambermaid, nor the incriminating residue left upon her sleeve by the venomous liquid. The subsequent farce of surprise, grief, and tragedy. I can see it all as if I had been there myself."

I could not counter the logic of his reasoning. But despite my grudging acceptance of his words, I could not quite bring my imagination to unite the delicate face of Victoria Valentine with the villainous portrait of a criminal such as Holmes described.

"Even so, Holmes; I cannot help but reproach you for your utter want of respect towards her when we met at the Stinking Wharf. It is hardly to be wondered at that she threw her pin at you in her shock and disgust."

Holmes laughed in his slightly sinister way. "Oh that," said he; "yes, that was altogether unexpected, wasn't it? She almost had my head nailed to the wall. But it was not complete disrespect on my part, Watson; it grieves me to say it, but that lady was as unworthy of our respect as she was reprobate in her actions. Both Cadbury and Nemo had been, I regret to say it, entirely hoodwinked and bewitched by that cunning and wicked woman."

"How can you even suggest such a thing, Holmes?" cried I, feeling both embarrassed for Holmes, and ashamed of him.

"Easily, Watson. On the day of our confrontation with Nemo, having gathered from the advertisements that the duo were accustomed to using the Stinking Wharf as a rendezvous and Poste Restante, I briefly visited the club in the early afternoon, intent on learning what I could of the habits of these particular patrons. With some metallic help that served to loosen the tongues of the resident servants, I confirmed that our angelic-looking little Miss Valentine was a frequent guest, and not only in company of the gentleman I described.

"What?"

"Since the moment of our first interview with Miss Valentine, I knew that she frequented that establishment, under the alias of 'Grim Vickie'. In fact, Grim Vickie and Captain Basil were old acquaintances."

"But who is Grim Vickie? I mean to say, what on earth..." I sputtered, utterly confused.

"Grim Vickie, to put it plainly, was a gentlewoman blackmailer; not long in the business, but already racking up points as a first-class crook. She always wore a black veil over her face—the very same veil you may recall seeing upon her delicate head when she passed by our table—and I, in my captain's guise, had observed her on more than one occasion plying her grim trade upon pale, frightened young girls. No doubt the latter were young ladies of her own social circle, against whom she held certain secrets. It so happened that I once sat quite near her table, and I overheard most of the conversation. It was not a very pretty one, I can assure you, and the terms presented to the desolated young victim were somewhat beyond steep. A short whispered conference with one of the waiters gave me the name of my veiled neighbor—Grim Vickie. It struck me, occupied though I was with pressing matters of my own, that a timely word from a hardened man of the world such as myself might put a bit of the fear of the Lord into this Miss Grim Vickie, whom I perceived to be a much younger lady than her apparel tried to suggest, and remind her of the straight and narrow.

126

With this purpose in mind, after observing the stormy departure of the victim, I rose and passed by her table, shooting, as I did so, a few sardonic remarks in the direction of her veiled ears. Her reply, though quite whispered, was stinging. After that we often bandied a word or two whenever we chanced to meet. I tell you, Watson, I can think of hardly anything quite as revolting as a respectable woman posing as a hard-cash blackmailer to the gentle, trusting members of her own sex. I had never had occasion to probe into her affairs, but I have had my eye on her all the same.

"During our interview with Mrs. Valentine it became obvious to me that she and Grim Vicky were one and the same person. Her manner and the rhythm of her speech, the slight tilt of the head – the evidence was instantly conclusive.

"Well, after the revelation of the matched identities, I set myself grimly to get to the bottom of the thing. I am not a very scrupulous man, Watson, when I am seeking for the truth. The seedy club Registry clerk consented, after he had pocketed 10 guineas of mine, to leave the room for five minutes, during which time I undid the flimsy catch and perused the contents of the lady's pigeon hole. It contained, as I suspected, the memoranda and memorabilia relating to a young lady's lucrative career in blackmail, including a detailed journal of every transaction made until that time, with notes on several that had not yet materialized."

I sank further into my chair, shocked and horrified at these further revelations of the wickedness of Miss Valentine's character.

"You may then well understand Miss Valentine's annoyance," Holmes continued, having sent a few contemplative puffs ceilingwards, "when she discovered that her shrewd one-eyed sea-captain acquaintance was really the well-known consulting detective Sherlock Holmes. I had expected some variety of emotion, but I had not imagined it would go quite so far as that ridiculous attempt on my life. From her point of view, it must have seemed like the last sporting chance. Alas, Watson, that her rashness should have led to her own death."

I knew Holmes spoke the truth; yet he must have perceived lingering traces of incredulity in my expression, for he sighed deeply and sank his frame deeper into his armchair.

"I take no pleasure in unearthing such wretched truths, nor in having to expose them. Do you know, Watson, it is probably just as well that Miss Valentine shall never now be called to face a panel of our solid English jury, who may easily have acquitted her, or at least lightened her sentence, on the strength of her delicate complexion, despite my testimony and the proofs of her guilt. As she is now in the presence of a Higher Tribunal, where we must each someday give account of our actions, let us now turn our minds from all woeful thoughts, Watson, and attempt to soothe our spirits with a refreshing strain. Hand me my old violin, will you?"

Listening to the haunting tunes issuing from the instrument, my thoughts were steered away from their melancholy moorings, and I was reminded that Holmes had once again taken a jumbled series of grotesque happenings, and, divining the vital facts from the negligible, had succeeded in throwing the light of truth upon the whole affair.

Arthur Cadbury, for example; though I had nearly forgotten about him of late, my heart was warmed by the realization that, thanks to the untiring efforts of my friend, the late young gentleman's honor was fully restored, and his country, which had so hastily jumped to slanderous conclusions at the start of the affair, would now hail him a hero and a martyr. *Who but Holmes*, I mused, my admiration growing every moment, *could have discovered the truth behind the all the smoke-and-mirrors?*

# Arthur Cadbury

# Chapter Eight

Mycroft Holmes called at our flat at around three o'clock the following afternoon.

"Brother Sherlock, Doctor Watson," said she, "I must firstly proffer my most earnest thanks to both of you. Your assistance and efforts in this perplexing and devious case have not by any means been unappreciated."

I bowed my head slightly in humble acknowledgement of her thanks. Holmes appeared to be in a doze.

"I'm sorry I could not come in last night, Sherlock," continued the lady, addressing her brother. "I was unexpectedly summoned to Windsor. I wished you could have accompanied me. However, despite her Majesty's profound gratefulness for your participation in this case, she expressed a certain disappointment at our lack of positive achievement so far."

From deep within the cushions of Holmes' chair came a sonorous laugh. Holmes' figure, following the sound, emerged suddenly from the cozy depths, and made for the large plate of sandwiches Mrs Hudson had sent up with tea.

"Too bad," said he, in between mouthfuls. "I do hope you informed her gracious Majesty that the matter is not yet closed, sister Mycroft."

"Indeed, Sherlock, that is precisely what I did not do."

"Why on earth not?"

"Because if we are to follow the trail which has been laid out before us, we must not be hampered by insignificant details, still less by official recognition.

If we admit defeat, that is, that the submarine plans are lost to us forever, we can then continue our investigations uninhibited by the usual pressures of state and Empire. If we locate the Engine cards in the process, well and good. If not, which is the more likely, we shall at least have the satisfaction of probing these fresh circumstances to their depths."

"True," said Sherlock, brightening. "My dear sister, I really must congratulate you. What is the recovery of a few Engine cards in light of the plot we have caught wind of?"

I admit that my confusion grew increasingly during the exchange between brother and sister.

"Now just a minute, Holmes," I broke in, "what's this all about? What plot? Whose plot?"

"Ah, that is what we must discover, my good Watson," replied Holmes, taking up another sandwich. "But if my sister is correct, and I am prepared to bet all my worldly goods that she is, this little case we have undertaken to solve is a mere song-and-dance routine masking the surface of a great cauldron of mysterious doings. Our friend Pierre Nemo, alias Peter von Oberon, alias Pierrot, revealed rather more to me than he might have otherwise, had he known better." Holmes finished his sandwich and retrieved his pipe. "I wish I knew where to find him now."

"It would surprise me greatly to learn that he is not, in fact, dead," I remarked. "In my opinion, the destruction of his getaway ship happened much too swiftly to allow anyone on board to escape."

"I would give much to know that for certain, Watson," said Holmes, tapping his pipe stem against his teeth. "He may have parachuted to safety amidst the falling debris. And after all, we do not know if he even boarded the ship. That man we saw fleeing the gurney could have been a decoy. If so, Nemo might easily have escaped to freedom. This case has had several features of interest, and this latest is the most interesting of all. Is Nemo dead, and if he is not, where is he now?"

"That will soon be ascertained," said Mycroft Holmes. "Already our international agents have been set to work researching his known contacts and tracing his past history. We know that he attended university in Berlin as Peter von Oberon, and subsequently took employment as an international agent for Moriarty Industrial; the name 'Pierre Nemo' has not yet appeared on any register at our disposal. But we are placing our sensors in every crevice imaginable, and if he is alive, we shall know it before long. Here we must deeply lament the loss of Sir James Valentine; he knew more about Nemo's ancestry than any other. His assistance would have been most invaluable to us at this juncture."

"What about the Rajput warriors that were captured?" Holmes asked. "Have none of them squealed?"

"The police haven't been able to get them to speak a word, yet," said Mycroft; "at least not in a language anybody in Christendom understands."

"The sacred tongue of the Rajput order," said I. "It is passed down from father to son, and taught to no outsiders, save only select students of their arts."

"I have no doubt that your people will tickle an English-speaking nerve before long," said Holmes dismissively. "Or perhaps one of your men could acquire the necessary fluency by becoming apprentice to another Rajput band in North India. In the meantime, there are other tracks to follow."

"What tracks?" I asked.

"Several are open before us, and one is most promising. The submarine designed by the original Nemo contained some very interesting articles of machinery, which must have been made upon specific order by some unsuspecting manufacturer. Most likely the Captain selected a different provider for each piece of equipment, so as not to arouse untimely suspicions, and it follows that each piece was ordered under a different name; however, there must have been a point of convergence someplace, which, when traced, must lead to the center of our spider's web."

"But Holmes," said I, "you said that the stolen submarine plans are inconsequential compared to the new plot you have unmasked. What then is the purpose of tracing the origin of equipment built over twenty years ago?"

Holmes looked towards his sister, who, after a short contemplative pause, undertook to reply.

"The Nautilus was a technological miracle from end to end," she said. "Its steam generator for internal systems and propulsion remained a complete mystery to our experienced Navy builders and scientists, even after two years of intense study; the steam engine used to propel the submarine was powered neither by $H_2O_2$, nor coal, but by something entirely different. There was a complete electricity-based auxiliary system, but the submarine's truly marvelous feats of prowess were apparently performed under the influence of some energy quite unknown to us. The team in charge of rebuilding the submarine were, of course, aware of this problem. The plan was to build the submarine exactly according to the plans, and use the auxiliary electric system to power the vessel until its main power source could be properly researched and defined. Sir James argued that, once the ship was built and in motion, a better understanding of its mysterious workings could be obtained. However, now that we no longer possess the ability to recreate this marvelous machine, we are faced with a series of staggering questions. What exactly is this new energy that we know nothing of? When was it discovered? Who discovered it, and how? How did Nemo acquire his knowledge, if indeed he did not discover it himself? What are its limitations? If such a powerful agent of force can be used to sustain a submarine, to what other ends can it be employed? Did Nemo alone possess the knowledge of its usage? I, for one, do not think he was alone in his knowledge. If there are others, who are they, where are they, and most importantly, what do they intend to do with this power?"

Understanding began to dawn on me as I listened to Mycroft Holmes' words. I uttered an exclamation of wonder.

"But this inquiry will be a colossal undertaking. It may take years!"

Mycroft Holmes smiled gently. "That is undoubtedly true, Dr. Watson. The investigation of this affair cannot be rushed along, for it promises to run a great deal deeper than we can even imagine at present. Fortunately, we do not lack for clues to help us direct our search, and I have every faith in the agent I have employed."

"Yes, it proposes to be by far the most interesting problem I have ever undertaken to tackle," said Holmes, complacently sending reels of blue smoke curling heavenwards. "It will be a refreshing diversion from the humdrum routine of my career of late. Petty crimes, committed by petty criminals, with petty, uninteresting minds. So few of my cases these days rise out of the commonplace morass of human indecency, greed, and pettiness. Even this Nemo, who at first interested me greatly as a specimen, proved himself to be a great deal duller than I had at first given him credit. And as for Miss Valentine..."

"A scheming minx," said Mycroft Holmes, rising from her chair. "Reprehensible in all her ways. Heaven knows she did a great deal of damage in her short lifetime. Thank goodness we need trouble ourselves no further on her account. Well, Sherlock, you will hear from me again soon. Good-bye."

\* \* \*

During the months following our adventures in the case of the stolen Engine cards, the tenor of our lives was not significantly altered, though Holmes often went out on solitary excursions that sometimes lasted up to several days, and he refused a good many clients. His energies, it seemed, he reserved for the strange web of mysteries which he and his sister had stumbled upon, surrounding the origin of the Nautilus submarine, and he diligently followed up every line of inquiry he could get hold of, though he was uncharacteristically taciturn in his conversations with me on the subject. It was all I could do to get him to speak of the matter at all.

The missing Engine cards did not resurface, and the Navy was unable to build its Nautilus submarine. The various deaths associated with the theft were explained away in a satisfactory fashion to the hungry masses of the nation, and, for which I was truly grateful, no mention was made of the devilish suspicions surrounding the late Victoria Valentine.

Her death was attributed to a tragic accident, which, though lamented by the public, nevertheless was considered a merciful occurrence, in the wake of her brother's death, and that of her fiancé Arthur Cadbury. That latter was, as I thought he would be, hailed as a worthy example of true bravery, a hero whose life was willingly sacrificed in the service of his country. No mention was published of Peter von Oberon.

This affair is a matter now of history—that secret history of a nation which is often so much more intimate and interesting than its public chronicles.

# P.C. Martin

P.C. Martin grew up traveling the world with her parents and speaks four languages including English, French, Spanish, and Portuguese. P.C. is a big fan of Sherlock Holmes, Steampunk, Star Wars, classic literature, and freely admits to being a Geek. She lives in the "Paris of South America", Buenos Aries, Argentina.

# Also from
# MX Publishing

Dozens of new novels, short stories and biographies of Sir Arthur Conan Doyle, from one of the largest Sherlock Holmes publishers in the world. Winners of the 2011 Howlett Literary Award (Sherlock Holmes book of the year) for 'The Norwood Author'.

Including the bestsellers:

The Lost Stories of Sherlock Holmes
Sherlock Holmes and The Whitechapel Vampire
My Dear Watson
The Secret Journal of Dr Watson
Sherlock Holmes and The Plague of Dracula
Sherlock Holmes and The Lyme Regis Horror

and many more at www.mxpublishing.com

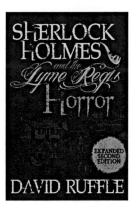

CPSIA information can be obtained at www.ICGtesting.com
Printed in the USA
BVOW011526130612

292547BV00002B/3/P

9 781780 922461